*A
Harlequin
Romance*

OTHER
*Harlequin Romances*
by MARGERY HILTON

# THE BEACH
# OF SWEET RETURNS

by

## MARGERY HILTON

HARLEQUIN BOOKS    TORONTO
WINNIPEG

Original hard cover edition published in 1975
by Mills & Boon Limited


SBN 373-01950-5


Harlequin edition published February 1976

Printed in Canada

# CHAPTER ONE

THE storm was almost over. The glistening bullets of rain were ceasing their bombardment of the drowning garden, and the fierce cascade down the veranda awning had dwindled to sulky, intermittent trickles. The sun stabbed through a cleft in the black clouds, and across the garden, beyond the ghostly burnish of a Shower-of-Gold, the big rain tree shivered beneath its heavy cloak of moisture, as though uncertain whether to open its tightly folded leaves to those stabs of warm vivid orange before it enfolded its green mantle against the approach of night.

Amber light spilled from the low sprawling bungalow and outlined in the doorway the slender figure of a girl with raven-dark hair. She stood immobile by the screen she had pushed open, her calm, oval-sculpted face betraying no fear at a sudden dimming of the light in the room behind her and the renewed thunderous reverberation of the storm's dying fling. The lamps flared back to full life and her shadow deepened across the veranda. Silence returned, to be gradually absorbed in the ceaseless small sounds of a tropical night: the stir of wings, the whir of ceiling fans, the miniature tattoo drummed by the tails of the tiny chik-chaks that clung to the walls ... the nights were merely degrees less noisy than the days.

The setting sun was swallowed again within the dark bank of the western sky, and Kate sighed softly, brushing gently at the papery wings of a large insect that had alighted on her arm. Her expression was unconcerned at the sudden fluttering swish of the insect's flight across her brow, and only the movement in the room behind made her turn her head.

Brad Sheridan set down his glass with a sharp movement. He stood up.

"Doesn't anything ever shake you, Kate?"

She smiled faintly. "If you mean, am I frightened of storms, no."

She felt the slight vibrations of the floor under his deliberate tread and willed herself to betray no tremor of tension as his hands closed lightly on her shoulders.

"I wasn't meaning storms specifically," he said.

"No, I didn't think you did."

His thumbs feathered lightly at the edges of the thin silky shoulder straps of her dress and slightly increased their pressure as he drew her back against him. His chin touched her hair. "You have a strange immunity about you, Kate. What's the secret?"

She kept her arms relaxed at her sides, remaining cool and immobile within his hold. "Is there any secret about immunity?" she said lightly. "One either gains it through suffering the complaint or takes steps to attain it artificially."

"Not your kind of immunity. I'm beginning to be convinced that it's genuine. Built-in, should I say?"

"Do you need convincing?"

"When it concerns a woman – yes. I can't believe in you, Kate."

"Is it necessary that you should?" Her voice gained a deeper inflection.

"No, but it's rather curious."

Her brows arched, but she stayed silent, half of her wary of him, the other half detached, listening for the sound of her father returning home.

Brad said in the same quiet tone: "You've been here a couple of weeks now, exactly three days less than me, which should put us on a kind of par. Within a few days I knew everybody at the club, and discovered that Mahore's European community is exactly the same as all the others dotted round this part of the globe. With exactly the same preoccupations," he added dryly.

"How boring you must be finding us, then," she said flippantly. "But it should be making it very easy for you to complete your dossiers."

"What do you know about my dossiers?" His tone was still deceptively light, but there was a subtle hardness behind the question.

6

Her shoulders moved. "Nothing."

"You made it sound so dramatic. As though I were an agent for CIA or something."

She ignored the amusement he put into the words. "Well, aren't you working along a certain similar principle?"

"Hardly – and stop sidetracking."

She turned her head sharply. "Oh, I thought the interrogation was over, and you – "

"Not quite." With the deceptive speed of expertise he moved, taking advantage of her momentary lapse of guard to turn her within his hands. "I've a great deal yet to discover."

The open screen was now brushing her back. To her left was a small veranda table which the boy had forgotten to bring in, and before her was the broad, arrogant strength of Brad Sheridan, suddenly alarmingly invincible. Kate's mouth compressed. She had few illusions, and escape was going to entail a certain surrender of dignity – the table was rickety and flimsy and would probably collapse if she tried to travel that way! and she had not yet attained the magic ability to melt through more solid barriers. All that remained was to duck quickly, or . . .

She stiffened. If he was determined to go on making passes she would just have to suffer; if it gave him any satisfaction to amuse himself with an iceberg he should have it, and welcome. Maybe he would take the hint in future. She looked up at the darkly handsome face and said coldly: "Is this part of the time and motion method as well?"

His mouth quirked unwillingly. "Not at all. I'm off duty! And when a girl stands alone, communing with a storm, it's very tempting to construe it as an invitation."

"Your construe is atrocious, then."

"And you are very sparing with your invitations, Kate."

His dark head blotted out the room and with cool deliberation he took her lips. Both the kiss and the caress which accompanied it were calculated, making no pretence about the expertise of their donor or their challenge, but there was something about his style that got straight through to feminine susceptibility . . .

7

Kate steeled herself against the small traitorous weakening and an unexpected pang of disillusion. Beneath her reserve she knew she was not an iceberg by nature and she was honest enough to admit that Brad Sheridan was extremely personable and far from lacking in male magnetism. But she preferred to make her own running, when *she* wished.

She looked up into his shadowy eyes as he drew back and said coolly: "You wouldn't guess why, of course, Mr. Bradley Sheridan."

His brows lifted with a trace of humour and he gave a small shake of his head. "I'm giving you the benefit of the doubt — maybe you're just shy, Miss Katrina Merrivale!"

He rested the back of one hand under her chin, quite gently, as he spoke, then let it stroke down the creamy column of her throat, before he added softly: "I wonder if you're so different, after all."

The sensuous caress made her more aware of him than his kiss had, and her composure wavered suddenly with the mainspring of anger. She bowed her head jerkily, looking pointedly at the strong tanned hand where it lingered, and her voice came out husky with mortification. "I'm neither shy, nor in the habit of angling to be pawed. And if you mean what I think, that by being different I am *not* one of the sex-hungry females who develop the tropic itch five minutes after coming out East, then make no mistake about it, I most certainly *am* different!"

She shouldered past him, uncaring of the shutter edge grazing her shoulder and rasping at the fine silk of her dress, and snatched up her emerald stole. She threw it about her shoulders with an unconscious betrayal of defence and said raggedly: "You can close the screens as you go."

"In a moment." His voice was unconcerned. "You're surely not throwing me out before I finish my drink?"

She compressed her lips, but made no response, hearing him move behind her. Ice clinked in a glass and a syphon hissed, then he came to her side, unhurried, the freshly mixed drink held like a further challenge in his hand. She turned away from the invitation.

"If it's whisky I don't want it."

8

"It isn't – nor gin. I've learned that much about you."

Unwillingly she took the proffered glass and sipped at the iced lime and soda, ironically as perfect a blend as she'd have fixed for herself, long, cool, sharp ... If only he would go! It was infuriating that he should have this power to ruffle her composure, even though he had not yet completely robbed her of her ability to maintain an outward calm.

Not for the first time she was grateful for the three arduous and exacting years she had spent modelling; the poise and assurance her training had imparted had their uses in other situations than those in the salon or under the camera's pitiless eye. She took another sip and reached into the green opaline box for a cigarette. The flame of Brad Sheridan's lighter sprang to life at the same time as that of the table lighter she flicked, and she made a small impatient gesture as he forestalled her attempt at independence.

"You shouldn't, you know," he said flatly, as she replaced the big lighter.

"Why not?"

"A bad habit rapidly becoming unfashionable."

"I've spent the last three years of my life being fashionable," she responded coolly. "Now I'm on holiday. Any objection?"

"Not to your being on holiday." His brows twitched slightly. "But maybe to smoky kisses from my women."

Her mouth compressed with anger and almost without realising what she was doing she stubbed out the cigarette so fiercely it snapped in two in the crystal ashtray.

"I'm not one of your women!" she flung at him. "Now, I'm afraid you're going to be unlucky – or have a hell of a long wait. The storm must have prevented my father getting back. He's almost certainly staying to dine with Marlow. So there's no point in your waiting any longer."

"I'm in no hurry." He gave no indication of annoyance at her outburst, or of noticing that at last he had succeeded in breaking her control. He walked calmly to the veranda door and drew the screens shut against the night. Then, as though with afterthought, paused with his hand on the latch and quirked

9

an enquiring brow at her. "Unless you change your mind and take the night air with me?"

"I'm not caring about the night air."

"So I've noticed."

She shrugged and dropped into a chair with the smooth grace which had become automatic. "Since this is only the second time you've paid me the compliment, my refusal can hardly be classed as a precedent."

He picked up his drink, his expression giving no hint of his thoughts. "Not yet. I trust it won't. Are you joining us this weekend?"

"I haven't decided yet."

"Scared of roughing it a bit?"

"That would be my last reason for refusing the trip." Abruptly she reached for her glass, almost wishing it was something more nerve-restoring than lime and soda with a dash of lemon and tinkling chips of ice. Why did it always have to be like this with Brad Sheridan? Always this verbal sparring and the need for a defence like the Great Wall of China? Why had she sensed it would be this way within five minutes of their first meeting?

Kate's mind flipped back to the evening of her arrival. Despite her unease about her mother's forthcoming surgery she had experienced a deep surge of exhilaration to be back in the East after so long an absence. To her surprise, she had recognised a nostalgia she would not have credited in herself during the years in London. Her self-possession had ebbed in this joyous feeling of homecoming and she had given way to excited recognition of landmarks remembered and exclamations at the changes time had wrought since her last visit.

Five years was too long, she had thought guiltily, even though she had settled into a working life in London with almost unbelievable ease. They had bridged adolescence and maturity, and they slipped by with unnoticed speed as she forged ahead in a successful career and the satisfaction of leading an independent life of her own. Not that this meant she loved her parents any the less; she had believed them equally happy, content to return to their own special relationship of two, a relationship whose felicity she had never had cause to doubt.

They in turn had known that Aunt Rena, her mother's elder sister, was there in Kent, to keep an eye on the youthful Kate stretching her wings and offer a friendly family hand should it ever be needed. But those five years *had* in a sense weakened family ties even as she was unaware of it happening, until the last two letters from her mother with their underlying note of worry made her realise just how far her life had diverged from the one so far across the world.

She knew she had not imagined the fervency in her mother's relief when all the arrangements were completed and she was coming home for three months. She knew also that she had done the right thing, despite the two very plum assignments she had been forced to turn down, when she finally stepped down into the familiar torrid heat and the never-to-be-forgotten smell of the East and sensed the burden of worry easing on her mother's shoulders. Yes, it was wonderful to be home again, even though she still privately considered that her mother's fears concerning her beloved father were groundless, and in spite of Brad Sheridan.

Kate's eyes narrowed slightly. That first evening when her father proudly escorted her down to the club in Mahore – "To show off my beautiful daughter" – and she had met Brad Sheridan she had wanted to like Brad, candidly admitting to herself that if she had met him back in London he would have been her kind of man and she would have enjoyed crossing mettles with him, even the indulgence in a lighthearted affair. But not here. The involvement in her father's working affairs precluded that, and the other fact which became obvious that very first meeting.

Brad was blatantly eligible; and he knew it. Kate thought of Elaine, and the young widowed Fay Slessor, and had no desire to align herself alongside them. Thank heaven she'd never been cursed with blinkers where men were concerned. Brad Sheridan didn't want her any more than he wanted the others, except for those moments when it amused him to play thrust and parry. He was the kind of man who would always make a woman forget her good resolutions, and Kate had no intention of ever letting herself get caught on any man's string again. She had learned her lesson two years ago when Ken Lester walked into her life, and her heart, a man like Brad Sheridan, possessed of an arrogant charm and the unfailing ability to walk on to pastures new, taking a girl's heart with him and leaving nothing in return ... No, if Elaine and Fay were prepared to make no secret of their willingness to sate his moments of boredom that was their affair, but not for her. So why couldn't he leave her out of his reckoning?

She glanced up and found him studying her with a level gaze she still found disconcerting.

"What's the matter, Kate?"

"Nothing – why should there be?" She kept her voice light and gave a careless shrug.

"I'm asking you."

"And I'm telling you. What more do you want me to say? Confide all my personal worries to Mahore's new avuncular trouble-shooter?"

"That's both childish and unfair, and you know it. I have a job to do," he returned equably, "like anyone else. There's something wrong with Mahore Latex's Sunei Batang sector and I have to put it right. It's as simple as that."

"Well, I can hardly have anything to do with Mahore's troubles, imaginary or otherwise," she said tartly.

"I didn't think you had," he said in cool tones. "But it does occur to me to wonder if you're afraid to come out from under the shelter of your father's wing. After all, you're a big girl now, Kate."

Stung, she glared at him. "That's too ridiculous even to merit an answer."

"Is it?" He straightened from his nonchalant stance by the screens, then added deliberately: "Maybe it's the other way about."

For a moment his meaning escaped her. Then her head turned sharply with shock. "An equally ridiculous supposition," she cried. "I'm not my father's keeper. Nor is he mine."

She set down her glass, aware that its ring was as hollow as her disclaimer. The unease he could evoke in her rose again, heightened by resentment and a strange twinge of fear that he could be so perceptive, as well as audacious enough to voice his suspicions.

She said icily: "Listen, my mother went to England last week, to have a very delicate eye operation. It's the first time in twenty-three years my parents have been apart. And it's also the first time in five years that I've spent an extended holiday with my father. We're finding a great deal to talk about and a desire to draw close, which is natural considering the circumstances. But perhaps that aspect hasn't yet occurred to you."

"It was one of the first to do so." His mouth was firm with the cool response, and his gaze deliberate.

"Well, I fail to see what it has to do with you," she said with a flash of defiance.

"Everything to do with the people who work for my company concerns me."

"But I don't work for your company – or you!"

"No, but your father does. And so does Walt Marlow."

Kate bit her lip. What in the name of heaven did Walt have to do with it? Suddenly weary, she got up and put her glass on the black lacquer tray, then she turned and faced her tormentor squarely.

"Just what is the meaning of this inquisition? Apart from the fact that this is an intrusion into my personal life. If it's all so vital, and you can't wait to discuss it with my father, I suggest you blow over to Walt Marlow's place and get it settled."

His brows went up. "That's quite an idea. I might – if you'll come over with me."

"No. I don't want to."

He gave a slow nod of his head. "Of course, you don't like Marlow, do you?"

"That's my privilege." She looked away. Was there anything that escaped Brad Sheridan's notice?

He moved around, until he could see her face again. "You believe in using your feminine privileges to the full, don't you, Kate?"

"It's scarcely taking advantage of a privilege to reject unwanted invitations."

"Mine as well as Marlow's, it seems."

She shook her head, suddenly abandoning the fight. "Please, Brad . . . I'm tired. I – I think it's reaction or something, or I'm not re-acclimatised yet, but something's hit me tonight. I wanted an early night, that's why I don't feel terribly sociable. It's nothing personal, honestly."

He nodded, his mouth compressing as he stood silent a few moments, his gaze searching her pale features. Then imperceptibly both his expression and his tone softened. "Kate . . ." he made a movement towards her, "just tell me one thing. Is anything worrying your father?"

"No!" She realised she had hesitated a second too long before the emphatic denial. "Nothing's worrying him, except the matter of my mother's sight. Apart from that he's fine. He just wants to know it's all over and have her back home. What else do you imagine could be worrying him?"

"That's what I was hoping to find out from you."

"My imagination isn't as highly trained as yours." She gave an elaborate shrug and reached for another cigarette. This time he made no move to supply the light, and when she had lit it she turned back to him, forcing a smile. "So will you excuse me, please? But if you would like to hang on a bit longer please feel free to do so. Just make yourself at home until my father gets back. I'm sure he won't be very late."

He shook his head. "No, I can take a hint if it's thrown at me hard enough. But thanks all the same for the afterthought." He picked up the folder of papers he had left on the coffee table and moved to the door. "I might look back later, but if not, tell your father I called."

"I'll probably be in bed by then, but I'll tell him in the morning."

Brad sighed. "Okay, it'll keep till tomorrow, anyway. So long."

She watched him stride down the waterlogged path to his car. The headlights snapped on and glistened across the ghostly cascade of white oleanders, outlining the dripping shrubs at the far side of the narrow track. For a moment the dark shape of Brad's head and shoulders turned, as though he stared back at the slender, pale-clad figure standing motionless in the shadows of the veranda, then one hand was raised in a brief salute before the low-slung convertible roared into life. Only when the red tail spots disappeared round the bend of the track did Kate turn to move indoors, and her outward self-possession fell from her like a discarded cloak. *What would keep until tomorrow?*

She dropped the latch on the screen and went slowly into the living room. She picked up his glass, set it on the tray, and her hand reached for the Bols, only to drop back to her side. No, that was one vow she had made when she returned out East and she wasn't going to break it, least of all for Brad Sheridan. Even though they'd all laughed at her parsimony over the drinks she allowed herself. She would succumb to the tipple the way they all did, they'd told her. It was something to do with the climate and lassitude ...

Kate sighed irritably and refilled her own glass with lime juice; for the first time tonight she had had a brief insight into how easy it would be to turn to alcohol.

Brad Sheridan's presence seemed to linger on in the room, disturbing and fraught with a sense of threat she could neither define nor dismiss, no matter how she attempted to reason with her silly fancies. Kate shook her head impatiently and wandered restlessly across to the book shelves, glancing along them at old remembered favourites with an unseeing eye. She knew a sudden temptation to seek her lipstick, as though it might dispel *that* little aspect of a provoking incident. But she thrust away the small impulse and tried to forget that her mouth still felt blurred and vulnerable from his kiss ... what did a kiss mean these days ...

Maybe if she'd played Brad along a bit more encouragingly he might have been a trifle more indiscreet; or if not indiscreet then a little more expansive about the real reason for his presence in Mahore.

She frowned. Business analyst/financial controller. That was the official appellation applied in the directive which had warned the Sunei Batang sector of Mahore Latex of Brad Sheridan's imminent arrival. A few of the younger hands in the firm had smirked behind their hands, and not a few acid comments about high-flown, new-fangled executive jobs masquerading under the guise of equally high-flown business jargon had circulated among the personnel, especially among the older hands who now constituted a very small proportion of the staff since Sunei Batang had come under the umbrella of the parent company. But a few of those, old in service who remembered the old days, like Kate's father, and Walt Marlow, and old Ah Weng, who had been part of the many small individually owned plantations that dotted the territory, knew that Brad Sheridan was here for a purpose.

They also knew that Brad Sheridan had been in rubber all his life, that he had been born and reared on his father's plantation in Malaya, to which he returned for five working years after the completion of his education. Then he had joined Mahore Latex. Yes, Brad Sheridan at thirty-two was old enough to have learned the hard way, yet still young enough to adapt to the changing conditions in the politics as well as the technology of the world of rubber.

And how they had changed.

The mist of reminiscence softened Kate's eyes. It was strange that she and Brad had shared almost identical upbringings; the fact that all her early memories must be very similar to Brad's own should surely give them a bond of understanding. Did he ever regret the passing of the old private plantations, the one-man rulers of the steamy miles of thin grey trees scarred with brown incisions like sticky stripes of ribbon? It was all so different now from the old days when Sunei Batang – the plantation she always thought of as "ours" – had been owned by Matt Marlow, father of Walt, and her father had managed it for the man she had grown to know as Uncle Matt. It had stretched right up to Jake Frisby's place, where Ah Weng and Suki had worked a section that now took six to oversee, according to her father, and there had been a slow, warm peaceful kind of security then, as though the aftermath of the war and the changes brought by independence had by-passed them somehow. Kate had spent the first nine happy years of her childhood in the Dutch-gabled house a stone's throw from the new modern bungalow Uncle Matt had built when he brought his young second wife out to Mahore.

Kate sighed, trying to see back with adult eyes through the mist of childhood memories.

She could remember Leila Denton with vivid clarity, even though Leila's sojourn had been a brief one. No one knew what had happened to that marriage. Some had said that Leila was far too young to settle down with a man twice her age and on a remote plantation so far from civilization and the life she had known in Singapore. Some had guessed she found a thirteen-year-old stepson too difficult to cope with, others hinted that she'd only married Matt to escape a domineering father and a mother whose chief solace in life was other men. But whatever the reason it hadn't been strong enough to hold her to Matt.

The day after Walt's fourteenth birthday she had gone, taking all her personal possessions and every penny she could lay her hands on. She had stayed two days in the only hotel Mahore possessed in those days, and the tongues had wagged viciously. But whether there was any truth in the rumours of someone out of her past, or the secret assignation everyone suspected, remained a mystery never solved. For on the third day Leila drove away in a drunken fury from Mahore and tipped the car with herself in it over P'bhamg Batee. By the time someone reached the blazing wreckage it was too late.

The tragedy changed Matt into the quiet, saddened man Kate remembered. She was six years old when it happened, and consequently Leila remained a beautiful isolated face in her memory. Leila had once given her a huge half-full crystal flacon of scent to play with, and had laughingly promised to bring the small, dark-eyed Kate a big scent spray next time she went to Singapore. But Leila had never got back to Singapore . . .

And so the rights and wrongs of the affair were simply garbled snatches overheard, something separate from the vivacious young woman remembered. But Kate did recall Walt Marlow in completeness.

He marked the only cloud over an otherwise happy childhood. There had been something about the adolescent Walt which had repelled her as a child; now, fifteen years later, re-acquaintance with Walt the man, already thickening into flabby, premature middle age, did not cause her to change the opinion formed in childhood.

She frowned. Walt had been seventeen when she left to go to her grandparents in England while she finished her schooling. He couldn't be more than thirty-two, the same age as Brad Sheridan, but he looked ten years older, and twenty years more dissipated. He'd long since run through the money Matt had left, and he hadn't been able to sell out fast enough to Mahore Latex after Matt's death five years ago.

Kate shook her head. She couldn't fathom why her father bothered with Walt. They were poles apart as well as a generation, and even though her father and Matt had been very close friends it didn't mean that he had to transfer that allegiance to the son. Heavens! Surely he had enough of Walt at the office.

Abruptly she stood up and crossed to the phone. She had to do something to dispel this mood of unease.

A few moments later she gave an impatient exclamation. She might have known the line would be down again after the storm. Still restless, she sat down at the little bureau and re-read the airmail letter that had arrived that day from her mother.

Why had her mother betrayed so much anxiety about this trip to England? It wasn't fear of the operation itself, Kate was sure, nor was it the possessive anxiety some women professed when they had to leave husband and family to look after themselves for a short while. On the surface, the circumstances didn't really seem to warrant Kate's taking three months' holiday to come all this way to look after her father until Mrs. Merrivale had completed her convalescence and returned. After all, Kate's father was far from being one of those helpless men.

But the anxiety was real enough. Kate hadn't forgotten her mother's face the night before the plane trip. She had tried to be bright and uncaring, but the tension was there in the background. It was patent between the lines of the letter Kate stared at now. Oh, yes, she was enjoying meeting old friends again, but wasn't England cold? Yes, she had seen the specialist that morning, and he was fully confident that the operation would be completely successful, but he was glad she hadn't delayed any longer. Yes, she was glad now she'd finally made the decision, and she couldn't believe she'd only arrived thirty-six hours ago, it seemed like ages. But she was writing almost straight away, because she was longing to hear from Kate, to hear that everything was going all right, that things were going smoothly and the new man wasn't stirring up too much trouble for them all ... why *had* he been sent there, anyway? Everything seemed to be running all right before he came ...

The blue airmail sheet hazed and shimmered in front of Kate's eyes. What indeed? Abruptly she picked up her pen and reached for the writing pad. Of course everything was okay. What *could* go wrong? And why on earth should Brad Sheridan want to stir anything up? He was simply one of the new order of industry. Everything was done differently today. One had to remember the sacred name of progress! After all, it was one thing managing a small, privately owned plantation, another thing altogether when it became part of a huge combine. There were twice the staff there had been in the old days, new methods, expansion, but her father had taken it all in his stride as area manager. She had to remember that there were four other plantations in the area besides what had been theirs. And Brad Sheridan had to dig and ferret, collect data, make suggestions, make a show to justify his presence ...

Trying to assure herself as much as her mother, Kate completed a long letter, keeping it as light and affectionate as she could, and when it was finished she decided she might as well go to bed. It was getting late, and the thought of a cool shower and cool crisp sheets – though they didn't stay like that for long in *this* climate – was very inviting. After all, if her father wanted to play cards into the small hours with Walt Marlow, why shouldn't he? She wasn't her father's keeper ...

She was coming out of the shower, tying the girdle of her wrap loosely about her slim waist, when she heard the footsteps on the back veranda. They were slow, almost dragging, and she tensed, instantly wary. There was something furtive about the sounds, and suddenly she wished she had not sent Benny, the houseboy, off to console his girl-friend during the storm.

The steps ceased, and she wondered if she had imagined them; she ought to be used again to the quiverings and rustlings of the tropic nights. Then the steps sounded again and she shook off the trance of fearful imagination. She rushed to the screens and flung them open, and the sharp question died on her lips.

"Father!" She stared as the tall, slightly stooped figure turned and faced her, looking almost guilty in the shadows. She took a step forward. "Daddy, why on earth are you creeping around like – like a thief in the night? I nearly went for the poker – only we don't have one!" She laughed unsteadily, but the puzzlement was still in her eyes.

He came forward. "I'm sorry, Katy. I didn't want to disturb you. I was trying to be quiet."

"I was in the shower. I expect that's why I didn't hear the car." She closed the screens and tightened the girdle of her wrap. "Come on, you old night-rake. I'll make some coffee."

"That would be fine." He was shouldering out of his jacket and she could see only his profile, but somehow the impression of guilt still persisted. For a moment a crazy thought flashed into her mind: surely he wasn't letting Walt turn him into a gambler like Walt himself! Then shock at her own disloyalty chased the unpleasant thought; her father would never allow himself to be influenced in that direction. Hadn't Uncle Matt begged him to keep a steadying eye on his dissolute son? And even Walt himself had admitted it, in that cynical, jokey fashion that had always irritated her so much?

John Merrivale had turned to face her. "Were you all right tonight – I was a bit uneasy about you?" He subsided into a chair, looking at her anxiously and rubbing his face tiredly with one hand.

"I was fine – although I did try to phone you. But the line's down again. But I guessed you'd stay on at – Oh, Father!" She saw the faint flush and the heaviness in his face, and she gave an exclamation of affectionate chiding. "I do believe you're a little bit squiffy. Walt's brandy! You are an old disgrace."

He smiled sadly. "I'm not, darling. Look." With a placating gesture he extended his hands straight in front of her; there wasn't a suggestion of a tremor. "I had a spot of trouble with the carburettor halfway back. That's why I'm hot and bothered."

"I'll make that coffee." She touched his cheek and smiled as she passed him.

He was still sitting, his expression faraway, when she came back with the tray. "Looking after the old man?" he said with wry humour as he accepted a cup.

She nodded, her expression thoughtful as she watched him sip coffee strong and black the way he had always liked it. How had she not noticed, at least until tonight, how her father was ageing? But did that tired, worried look behind his forced humour have the perfectly natural explanation of time's passage? But her father wasn't old. Fifty-three wasn't a symbol of decrepitude these days. Abruptly, she leaned forward.

"Daddy, is anything worrying you?"

At the old affectionate childhood address he glanced at her sharply. After a pause he laughed and shook his head. "Worrying me? What makes you ask that, Katy?"

"Because I want to know. Apart from Mother's trouble, is there anything on your mind?"

"Of course not!" Hearty again, he had recovered from his surprise. "Except overwork and the cost of living."

"I didn't mean that." Already she saw defeat but something made her persist. "It's just instinct that made me ask. You look a bit ... You *would* tell me, wouldn't you? I mean, if it was health, or difficulties at work ..." she hesitated, "or just Brad Sheridan's throwing his weight about. He was here tonight, asking for you."

"Was he?" John Merrivale's voice sounded unconcerned – perhaps too unconcerned, Kate thought. "Is he worried about me as well?"

She bit her lip. If her father chose to be unforthcoming all the probing in the world would fail to bring the confidence she sought. She shrugged, and made one more effort. "He didn't say, but I got the impression that something was bugging him. Oh, Daddy, we've never had secrets in the family, so don't let's start now. Worries are for sharing. Right?"

"Right." He met her pleading gaze, then touched her arm. "No secrets. But please don't remind me of work until Monday, young lady. Whatever happens to be bugging our friend Brad will have to go on bugging him till then. We're going to enjoy ourselves this weekend."

"Are we?" She raised querying brows.

"The crowd is going up to the club's new place – I told you about it, remember? I said we'd join them."

When she did not respond he said quickly: "You haven't made other plans, have you?"

"No, but . . ."

"Then why the lack of enthusiasm? You used to love the lagoon, especially Dr. Lim's little stretch of beach. In fact, I'm surprised you didn't make a beeline for it the moment you got home."

"The Beach of a Thousand Sweet Returns . . ." Kate's eyes took on a musing light as memories temporarily banished unease. One of the many charms of Malaysia was the delightful choice of names for some of its more beautiful beaches. Some of them were frankly romantic, like the most famous of them – the Beach of Passionate Love on the eastern shore of Malaya – but others, like that on the northern shore of Mahore's lagoon, held a sweet nostalgia that could pluck the chord of memory. For Kate, this little beach had always been a special place, associated with the kind of happiness that instinct told her could never come again, simply because those tender years of childhood were long past recall.

Deliberately she severed the sentiment of memories. "I've stopped making sentimental pilgrimages, they usually bring only disillusion."

"It's still the same, Kate," her father said placatingly. "The new club place is on the southern side and hasn't detracted from the lagoon's natural beauty in any way."

"No, it isn't that." She sighed. "Everything is different now."

"Things are always different when one grows up," he said

quietly. "But it doesn't mean that one can't derive as much pleasure from them in a different way."

"Not the little beach." She put the beakers back on the tray and stared down at them. "I loved it because it was so wild and pagan and beautiful. I could run along it and pretend I was the only child in the world. Remember that storm? When we took shelter in the little shell summerhouse . . ." She looked up almost pleadingly. "Is it still there? And the white villa?"

Her father nodded. "It's getting overgrown now. Dr. Lim rarely comes back, not since his wife died."

"He used to tell me the names of all the shells that were stuck over the little summerhouse. The wife of the planter who originally built it had patiently gathered and stuck on all those shells. She'd picked out her name on the side in cowries. Victoria . . ."

John Merrivale smiled reminiscently. "You were a somewhat acquisitive six-year-old. Asking Dr. Lim if you could come and live in his shell summerhouse!"

"And he said yes." Kate smiled, then sobered. "Don't you ever dare tell the crowd. How they'd laugh at me! But I can understand his not wanting to go back. It's always a mistake to revisit places where one has known special happiness."

"True, but there's no reason why you shouldn't still find enchantment there, my dear."

She shook her head, her expression hardening. "Not if the crowd have made it their new playground. Somewhere to fool around, and drink too much, and flirt with each other's husbands and wives. No, Father, I've no desire to play with the club crowd. Or with Walt, or Brad Sheridan."

Her father's eyes had grown troubled. "I think it's time I asked what's worrying you, Kate. You've changed during the last few years."

"I don't think so." Her face shuttered.

"Oh, yes, you have. It was Ken, wasn't it? You've let one unhappy affair colour your opinion of all men. I know you've never hit it off with Walt, but he isn't the only man here. So why have you been so chary of accepting invitations since you came home? It's not like you to be stand-offish."

She gave a start of surprise. "I'm not! Whatever gave you that idea? Can't I refuse an invitation if I want to?"

"It's not that, and you know it," he said quietly. "Just because one man let you down you've put a shell round yourself and if a man won't play on your terms you won't play at all."

"You've noticed a lot about me in a couple of weeks, haven't you?" She tried to keep her tone light, even as she felt shock at her father's perception. "I never dreamt that my letters home carried so deep an impression of Ken Lester's effect on me. But I've almost forgotten him. What makes you think otherwise?"

"I've known you for twenty-two years, Katy. And when your letters suddenly stopped mentioning Ken, and didn't give a single hint at the reason, we knew something had gone wrong, but we respected your right to reserve your confidence. Then when we realised that you weren't mentioning any man's name at all, among all those parties and that mad whirl you seemed to live in . . ." John Merrivale paused, and made a weary movement with his shoulders as he looked at her with a level gaze. "We tried to tell ourselves that you were becoming self-assured and independent, and there was no reason to believe you were any different, basically, from our own little Katy. It wasn't until you were actually home again that we realised how hardened you had become in your outlook on life," he added heavily.

Kate had never heard such a long, analytical and frank appraisal from her father. For the moment she hardly knew what to say – unless she admitted how dangerously near the truth he had come.

"Oh, Daddy," she said helplessly at last, "surely I haven't changed as much as all that! I'm not hardened – only trying to protect myself against the hard cruel world! Every girl has to – today. Anyway, we were talking about *you*," she added quickly.

"And the weekend." He got to his feet, stretching lazily, and reached out to brush her cheek with the old remembered gesture of affection. The previous cross-challenges might never have been voiced. He smiled. "Who knows? Maybe tomorrow you'll find your rainbow."

Privately Kate doubted it. Her unease was not to be banished as easily as that. But it was obvious that her father had no intention of confiding in her – if there were anything to confide.

Kate returned his goodnight kiss and hoped that her instinct was playing her false. The trouble was, it so rarely did.

# CHAPTER TWO

"So you changed your mind after all."

Brad Sheridan dropped down by Kate's side and composed his broad tanned frame on the soft warm sand. He looked at her with frankly appraising eyes, obviously waiting for more response than the tiny lift of fine brows which was all she permitted in acknowledgement, and Walt Marlow grinned.

"It's a woman's privilege, old man," said Walt, in such banal tones that Kate winced. "All they need is a little persuasion. It's a woman's spice of life."

"I thought spice was something one cooked with," giggled Fay Slessor.

"Remind me to give you a cookery lesson soon," said Walt, and Fay giggled again.

Kate closed her eyes and feigned indifference. Already she was beginning to regret that change of mind. She should have remembered her vow about sentimental pilgrimages.

The lagoon was as beautiful as ever; her memory had played no tricks in that respect. The sun poured down on the limpid green oval within its encircling ribbon of beach and glowed on the rich verdancy of forest that held every tint of green leaf and fern imaginable. A soft breeze feathered the ripples lapping the shore, helping to temper the humidity, and now there was shade and ice-cold drinks almost within arms' reach when required.

Kate sighed. Despite her forebodings she had to admit that the huts the club had built in the clearing up the beach in no way blotted the natural beauty of the terrain – they could scarcely be seen until one broke through the circle of shrub and palm, so skilfully had their design been carried out – but she could not banish her sense of resentment when she let her gaze stray across the sparkling expanse to the scene of her favourite childhood playground. Her half-closed eyes traced the opposite shore, from the green tip where land met sea, along to the kampong and the site of the old clinic, now unneeded since the building of the new hospital along the new road, and then slowly along the thick belt of green until her gaze rested on the deserted sickle of silvery beach. She could just distinguish a corner of the white villa where Dr. Lim once lived, and the tiny shape to its left of the little shell house ... It looked so lonely now, nestling in its clearing under the palms, as though it waited for someone to return, a sweet return, but not the pleasure-seeking set from Mahore's club.

Abruptly Kate wrenched her gaze away, trying to reason with herself. She had no right to feel this irritation. The personnel had as much right to a place of recreation as herself, if not more. Thoughtfully, she studied her companions, seeking to discover in them the reason for her unreasonable reluctance to become involved in their brittle social life.

The most easily likeable was Fay Slessor. She was pretty, if slightly vapid, her little-girl act understandable when one considered her fragile, ingenue-blonde features and silvery sweet voice, but less so when one remembered that she was twenty-eight and widowed. Fay could be inane at times, and shallow, but at least she was honest, Kate thought. Fay made no secret of the fact that she disliked the state of widowhood, that her main interests were men and clothes, and her main objective the finding of a second husband. But she possessed a warm, friendly disposition that drew one to her instantly, which was more than could be said of Elaine Winton.

Elaine was a dark, sultry beauty with a built-in allergy to the rest of her own sex. This had become patent the first time Kate met her. Kate repressed the thought that it was a pity Elaine didn't spare some of the charm she evinced towards most men for her husband; it wasn't for her to share the surmise of the gossip-mongers at the club. But it was difficult not to surmise after an hour or so in the company of Elaine and Rex Winton. Even now, out in the sparkling water, they were quarrelling, or at least Elaine was trying to quarrel.

Kate's eyes narrowed as she watched the two figures. Everyone liked Rex. He was the most easy-going member of the set, placid, and always predictable. Perhaps that was what irked

Elaine, Kate decided. If Rex were to turn on his temperamental, selfish young wife and give her the spanking she deserved the shock might bring her to her senses.

"Oh God, she's started again," Fay muttered. "I could wring that girl's neck. Poor Rex! If I were he I'd give her hell."

Walt tittered. "Speaking as a mere man, I don't think you would, darling."

Fay gave him a disgusted glance and knelt down beside Kate. "Just because Rex wasn't keen on her going off with those high-flying friends of hers for a month she's making his life a misery. Of course it doesn't matter that Rex is due his leave in two weeks' time. I suppose he could sweat it out here until she got back from Melbourne. And what are *you* grinning at?" she demanded of Brad Sheridan.

Across Kate's unmoving body he looked at Fay's indignant face. "You, sweetie. It's so unusual to find a female who can see the poor downtrodden male's point of view."

Fay ignored the sarcasm in his voice and turned her attention to the girl in the scarlet bikini who was storming out of the water. Elaine ran up the beach towards the club-house doorway. The soft click-clack of the bead curtain ricocheted down its length as she thrust it aside, and Fay gave a muttered exclamation.

"Elaine!" she called. The slender figure paused and glanced back impatiently. Fay scrambled up. "Could I borrow your lotion? Mine's run out."

"Help yourself." Elaine's response was indifferent as, without waiting until Fay caught up with her, she melted into the shadows within.

Kate stirred uneasily on the warm sand. Suddenly she was unaccountably conscious of Brad Sheridan's strong taut body stretched out beside her, and the sight of Walt looking down at her with that unpleasant, pursed little smirk of his seemed to heighten that discomforting awareness.

Telling herself not to be ridiculous, Kate tried to ignore it and restrained a second glance at Brad, who was lying with his eyes closed, apparently oblivious to the small scene which had taken place. Fay would be back with that very expensive body lotion Elaine used and there would be the inevitable, even if unspoken, invitation to a volunteer to make the necessary application to Fay's shapely little shoulders and back. Why was it that the petite, coquettish girls seemed to command indulgent male attentiveness with scarcely batting an eyelash? For the second time within minutes Kate experienced a surge of irritation and a desire to be alone.

She sat up, and Brad's eyes flickered open.

"You as well?"

She stiffened warily. "As well what?"

"Leaving us?"

"I see no undue signs of anyone suffering." She sprang up, choosing not to see the hand Walt extended, and went fleetly down to the water's edge. Without breaking the smooth rhythm of her movements she splashed into the lagoon and slipped into a lithe overarm stroke that took her rapidly into deep water.

Kate was a strong and confident swimmer, and she knew there was no fear of Walt pursuing her into the water. He was too inherently lazy to be anything but an indifferent swimmer, and unless he had changed radically he wouldn't risk his skin where there was the remotest chance of sharks being present. Though he'd never admit it now, she thought cynically as she cleaved the cool silken ripples; but she still had clear memories of the pudgy boy who in bygone days was not so discreet about his fears. Nor did he differ from all other bullies in that the weak and the helpless invariably provided the target for his mean little ways; the strong and the predatory had no cause to fear him. Oh, forget Walt, she told herself crossly. She'd be foolish to allow her childhood fear of him to spoil her first visit to the lagoon for so many years.

She had almost reached the shallows where sandbanks narrowed the neck of the lagoon and she slowed, looking for the old landmarks to guide her way. Beyond a curiously shaped outcrop of rock was a section of reef that enclosed a deep and beautiful water garden. Was it still there? and the natural underwater archway which formed its gateway?

How often had she delighted in the plunge through the sea-green depths while her father stood above and watched the swift confident dart of her small, emerald-clad body! Strange that she should remember that vivid little swimsuit he had bought for her ninth birthday; she'd had many since then, and long since lost count of the exotic array she had modelled ... Smiling now, and Walt banished from her mind, she clambered up on to the rock shelf and shook the streaming rivulets from her hair. With volatile speed her mood had changed and a joyous sense of freedom had taken possession of her spirit. She dashed moisture from her eyes and stood poised, her head flung back as she revelled in the blazing sun and the idyllic scene surrounding her.

She could scarcely see the club-house from her vantage point, only a corner of its pale, coral-hued roof hidden under the arch of jungle foliage. The lagoon shimmered like a great oval emerald framed in silver-gilt sand and the gently swaying fringe of palms. Here, man might not exist, nor the problems life brought; here was a brief escape into the sheer sensuous beauty of nature during one of her rare benevolent moods.

A tall, slender figure of perfect grace, Kate picked her way along the ledge, realising she had forgotten one of the cardinal rules her father had instilled into her. But the reef was worn smooth here, free of the razor sharp protuberances which could cause serious cuts to unwary feet, and she reached the point above the pool safely, sighing a smile as she discovered that time had wrought no change.

It was exactly as she remembered it; the great curving bowl within the coral, the rainbow fish playing amid the waving clouds of sea fern, the dark and the light dappling the sea bed, and the fairy gates of coral that had fascinated her from the first moment of discovery. Such strange fantasies she had woven; of a sea naiad and her coral prince, and the dark enchantment of the gorgonian witch ...

For a moment longer she gazed down at the arch beneath the ripples, then she took a deep breath and dived deeply.

No fear was in her as the waters enclosed her and the magic green element took on its silent, unearthly luminosity. She came up at the other side, blinked at the blinding gold of the sunlight, and gulped in fresh lungfuls of air before she glided down into the return descent.

She sensed nothing, only the delicious sensation of being free in an alien element, until the great black shadow cut the water within feet of her. The dreaded thought: *shark!* exploded in her mind. Panic threatened to overcome all reason, all knowledge that the pool was supposed to be safe. Sharks couldn't get in: her father had taught her to swim here, bringing her out in the boat, and ... She kicked wildly, striking upwards, fighting to reach the surface before that deadly shadow turned.

She thought the gilded surface would never break about her head, and then, limbs threshing desperately, she was gasping and struggling towards the ledge where she could scramble to safety. There could be a break now. Wild storms could have breached the pool's barrier. Anything could happen in so many years. Whole coastlines changed ...

She crouched on the sunwarmed ledge and dashed water from her eyes as she stared down fearfully into the crystal water. Where was it? Or had she imagined it? She must have done – this beautiful pellucid pool had always been a swimmers' haven, as safe as any tropical pool could be judged by the word. Then she shrank back as she saw the rippling shadow, gasped aloud as she recognised it.

The sight of Brad Sheridan's head breaking the surface did nothing to lessen the trembling of her body, or appease the sudden surge of anger rushing through her.

"It was *you!*" she gasped.

"Who did you think it was?" He pulled himself up and flicked dark glistening brows at her.

Almost blurting out her fear and anger, Kate managed to check herself and remain silent. She pretended to be intent on squeezing water out of her streaming hair, and tried to steady her rapid breathing.

"You came out in a hell of a hurry," he observed dryly.

"Did I?" She didn't look at him.

"You certainly did," he returned. "Perhaps it's just as well I didn't give in to a very tempting temptation down there."

Her head turned and she stared wide-eyed.

His mouth curved mischieviously. "Just a spot of old-fashioned water sport! Those long legs of yours were begging to be grabbed."

His glance patently caressed the long slender limbs in question, and Kate felt the colour mount in her cheeks.

"But I restrained my ungentlemanly impulses," he went on, allowing his gaze to shift to the wavering outline of the coral portal beneath the ripples. "You might have taken fright and thought it was a marauding denizen of the deep."

"Idiot!" Her voice trembled, despite her tight lips. She was still too close to the shock she had suffered as his shadow overcast her in the depths of the pool to be able to dismiss his confession with a light retort. If he *had* given in to impulse and grabbed her legs as she swam underwater she would have panicked abominably.

"I suspect you were more scared than you're admitting," he said, after a further speculative survey of her. "Good job I wasn't Walt."

"Could you imagine Walt exerting himself to that extent?" she said coldly, bending to examine a beautifully marked shell clinging just below the water line. "Why do you think – ? *Oh!*"

He had walked hard cool finger-tips down her spine as she crouched, and she whirled upright, her eyes flashing anger. At her exclamation of annoyance he merely grinned unrepentantly, putting up his hands in a mocking gesture that feigned a plea for pax.

"Don't say it, sweet Kate." He backed a pace, still grinning. "I'll even apologise for my wayward hands – it'll be worth it."

"What do you mean?"

"To see you lose your cool for once."

Her spine still tingled from the touch of those wayward hands, and she flung a glance of dislike at him. "Does that really provide you with such immense satisfaction?"

"Not exactly." Glimmers of amusement made his eyes sardonic. "But it'll help to convince me of something next time I need that conviction."

She knew she was being deliberately needled, but she could

not help retorting: "I fail to see why you should need conviction, or convincing of anything where I'm concerned."

He shrugged. "We males are not entirely devoid of human curiosity, Kate."

"I've no secrets," she snapped.

"To me you have," he said coolly. "Simply the desire to discover that you are indeed a warm, living girl with the blood of emotion in your veins, instead of that iced water you develop for the camera lens."

"Aren't you being faintly ridiculous?" she mocked. "Ice? The blood of emotion? I would never have imagined you could be so fanciful!"

"There's a great deal you wouldn't imagine about me. Maybe you'd be surprised if you tried to find out."

"Small talk." She turned away and began to retrace her steps along the ledge. "It doesn't mean anything to me."

"It might if you added it up." He moved after her.

"Big libretto by Brad Sheridan!" Kate was recovering her composure now – or back inside her smooth professional shell within which she felt a great deal safer when he was around. She looked over her shoulder at him, trying to frame a retort that would penetrate that hard hide of his and chalk up at least one score to Katrina Merrivale. "Perhaps if you – *Oh* – !"

*"Don't move!"*

He had seized her in so violent a grip she froze with the pain of it.

"Don't put your foot down!"

The command was so forceful she obeyed without thinking, even as bewilderment succeeded the shock and pain of his interruption. His fingers bit into her arm and shoulder, still forcing her back in the frozen pose of arrested movement, then he said softly: "Just move back slowly, and look down."

Afraid now to move, even though the fear was inexplicable, she shook her head and stayed tense against him. Slowly she looked down, at the long uneven ledge, over which the lazy swell of the lagoon reached in slow, ebbing ripples. There was a shallow pool in a hollow, deeper at one side and petering into sun-dried reef at the other. Her next step would have splashed into it, but for Brad's sudden grab, and it took a second, closer look before she saw the reason for his fierce action.

It was a stone-fish.

Her blood ran cold as she stared down at one of the deadliest menaces of tropical seas. It lay there, quiescent, scarcely breaking the surface of the water, its rough wartlike scales a perfect camouflage against the bed of the pool, and the poison in its spines invisible, but invariably fatal. If she'd stood on it . . .

A gasp escaped her and she began to tremble violently.

"It's all right – we saw it in time." There was an indulgent note in his voice, as though he spoke to a scared child. "If you will disobey all the rules . . . Come on back, this way, where – "

She shook her head blindly as he drew her back, away from that silent menace waiting there, and protest was the last thing in her mind as he drew her trembling body into his arms. He pressed her face against his shoulder and stayed silent until she drew a deep breath and whispered:

"If you hadn't seen it I might – I might have – "

"I did see it. So 'might' didn't happen," he said gently. "Forget it."

"It's the first time I've ever seen one," she said unsteadily. "But I knew about them. Knew you should never walk barefooted on the reef. . . . But I forgot . . . I should have remembered. I – "

Her voice broke, and she looked up shakily into his face. She wanted to thank him, but did not know how to put gratitude into words which would not betray how utterly foolish and unnerved she felt. If he laughed it off her mortification would be complete. Yet he had almost certainly saved her life.

Her glance fell. "I don't know how to thank you. You – "

"Sweet Kate, I've told you – forget it!" Laughter shimmered along his mouth and narrowed his eyes. "You had a hell of a fright – but what about me!"

"You?"

His hands moved up and down her arms, then slid convulsively across her back. "Yes, me," he said, abruptly sober. "My imagination can work overtime the same as anyone else's. I guess I need to forget it too."

He stared down into her upturned face, into eyes still dark with the horror of what might have been, and his own eyes shadowed. Suddenly he pulled her hard against him and bent to her mouth.

Instinctively she closed her eyes against the glare of sky and sun. It seemed as natural as breathing to accept this subliminal reaction to horror. For long spinning moments she forgot she had ever feared or disliked Brad Sheridan. All she knew was a sudden rushing joy, a new awareness of life and being alive, alive in his arms and vibrant with the sheer male strength of him. There was a wild ecstasy in feeling the long hard pressure of his body against hers, until the fierce contact flowed into a warm fusion that almost melted her bones and left only the culminating heart of his kiss.

The world, time, space, everything, retreated. There was only the joy, and this wild throbbing response that carried her senses on an endless swirling crest.

"Oh ... Kate ..." His mouth moved roughly against hers and she did not know whether the great sigh shuddered through his body or her own.

She opened her eyes and the sun blinded into them, around the blurred outline of his head. The world rushed back, and she put up trembling hands to his shoulders, feebly trying to break that overwhelming contact. The gesture expressed not so much a defensive thrusting away of him but rather a staving off of her own sudden weakness. She averted her face and took an unsteady breath.

"We – we'd better get back."

"Must we?"

Without answering she disengaged herself from his hold and took a header into the water. As she came up she heard the splash of his following plunge, and a sudden urgency made her clip through the water at a speed she had not attempted for years.

She was breathless and still shaken when she came ashore, to the silent waiting group by the water's edge. The thought of their trivialities and the sight of their faces made her want to rush past, but Fay was standing right in her path. Dimly she sensed Brad's presence coming near, and with an effort she forced a careless smile.

But Fay did not smile in return. "Whatever happened to you out there?" she demanded.

"What should happen to me?" Kate parried, more curtly than she intended.

"*I* don't know." Fay looked hurt. "We just wondered. We could see you, and then Brad took off in a hurry, without a word, as though ... Well, we just wondered ..." She glanced at the others, as though for confirmation of her doubts, and Rex Winton nodded.

"That's right. But then the pair of you ended up looking so cosy we decided that a rescue party wasn't needed after all," he grinned.

"Marvellous eyesight – full six-six," Brad commented dryly, brushing water from his hair and placing his other arm casually across Kate's shoulders.

"Actually, we weren't sure who needed rescuing," said Elaine, with a sidelong glance at Kate.

"A difficult problem," Brad observed coolly.

Kate felt colour invade her cheeks. Walt was staring at her, his displeasure plain, and abruptly she ducked to pick up her beach bag.

"I nearly stood on a stone-fish," she said.

There was a silence, then, "Oh, God! You didn't!"

Rex's shocked exclamation sounded unnaturally loud. There was a murmur from Elaine and a gasp from Fay.

Kate had not intended to mention the incident. Not from any desire for secrecy but for the simple reason of sparing her father a worry that was now unnecessary. But at least the announcement proved a successful diversion from Brad's part in the scene, for which she was fervently thankful.

"Oh, it must have been *ghastly!*" Fay said impulsively. "Are you sure you're all right?"

Kate nodded, and Fay gave a shudder. "You must have been petrified. I know I would have been."

"I was," Kate admitted, trying not to listen to Rex's voice behind her as he recounted the story of someone he knew who had inadvertently trodden on one of the deadly fish and the sting had proved fatal.

Some of the peevishness had gone from Walt's face. He took Kate's arm. "You shouldn't have gone out there, hon. Come and have a drink." He began to steer her up the beach.

"I'm all right," she repeated, then checked her step, turning to look pleadingly at her companions. "Please . . . don't anyone tell my father. Promise?"

"Of course we won't," Fay soothed, and there was a murmured assent.

"After all, it's over now," said Elaine. "And who knows? You might never have stood on it. I mean, if you hadn't noticed it and just walked within an inch or two . . ."

"That's true." Kate's voice was a little curt as she stepped up on to the veranda of the clubhouse, where her father and Harold Parham, the club treasurer, were relaxing in the comparative coolness of the awning's shade. Lena and Tom Maddison, a middle-aged couple, were there, sharing iced drinks, and Kate took the chair her father drew forward between himself and Lena.

"You swim superbly, my dear," the older woman smiled, while Walt and Brad went indoors to fetch drinks.

"My daughter's always been a great little swimmer," John Merrivale said proudly. "Have you rediscovered the pool?" he asked, turning to Kate.

She nodded, suddenly aware that she was watching the doorway for Brad's reappearance. She bit her lip and made herself turn in her chair so that she faced into the little group. Was she forgetting so easily her conviction that Brad Sheridan had something to do with the lines of worry that had given her father's features their drawn look? Her unease, and that of her mother, surely couldn't be entirely imaginary? Yet despite this she had let herself respond to Brad's embrace, to his kiss . . . in a way that brought a quickening of her heartbeats and a warm inward surge of excitement at just the memory.

Yet how could she have helped her betraying weakness? Supposing he hadn't seen the peril that lurked almost invisibly in her path? What if his reflexes had failed to explode into action in time? For despite Elaine's cool little remark, danger had lain within inches. It couldn't be denied, even by trying to tell herself that it would never have happened if he hadn't followed her, that but for his advent she might not have been on that part of the reef, might not have relaxed that wariness her father had instilled into her since her babyhood days. It *had* happened, and she could never deny the dénouement that had changed her relationship with a man she disliked, whether she liked it or not.

The feeling of guilt and disturbance nagged at her during the rest of the weekend. She was not sorry when it was over and Monday morning found her alone in the bungalow after her father left for Mahore and the start of another working week.

He had seemed a little more cheerful, more his usual self, as he got into the car after dropping an affectionate kiss on her cheek and reminding her to take things easy.

She knew he wanted her to look on her stay as an extended holiday – and also that he considered her far too thin since adopting her successful career.

"I liked my rounded Katy, with her impetuous ways," he had remarked the night after her arrival. "The Katy who spoke before she thought and then giggled her way out of a gaffe."

"That Katy had to grow up," she had reminded him, and joy at the reunion had masked any trace of wistfulness that might have softened her tone.

He had smiled and sighed ruefully in response and it was at that moment she had decided the lines of worry etched round his eyes were not entirely due to overwork and concern about Mrs. Merrivale. It was then the conviction had grown that he had something on his mind, and she had begun to have insight into her mother's similar suspicion. But how to do anything if the cause of their concern had no intention of sharing his trouble was almost as big a problem. Kate sighed and wandered indoors, deciding to check the stores and see what needed ordering.

Benny greeted her with a friendly grin. He had been with the family for several years, and his mother, Ah Nuna, the dear old *amah* who had been like a second mother to Kate all through her childhood, had served Mr. and Mrs. Merrivale faithfully from the day they had arrived at Sunei Batang, all those years ago. Kate's mouth curved wistfully at her memories, then abruptly she put sentiment aside. She was doing far too much day-dreaming – positively wallowing in a sea of nostalgia ever since she got back, she decided firmly. It was time she started being practical for a change.

Over a cup of coffee she worked out the week's menu with Benny, and in her enthusiasm as she recalled her father's favourite dishes she did not notice Benny's smile vanishing, to be replaced by a worried frown.

"So we'll settle for *sates* on Wednesday, and his adored Peking Duck on Thursday . . ." Kate tapped the pencil against her teeth and stared across the big airy kitchen in search of inspiration. "He'll be eating with Walt on Friday," she went on slowly, "so I'll just have a put-off. Then – "

"Put-off?" Benny's smooth, Asiatic features slanted a little more with puzzlement. "What kind of food is put-off, mem Kate?"

Kate laughed. "Sorry, that's what my Aunt Rena over in England always says when she's just going to make a snack for herself instead of cooking anything. Now, where were we? Saturday is sacred to the club, but I refuse to go out anywhere on Sunday." She gave a sigh. "Actually, I think it's high time we gave a dinner party, we've quite a few invites to return."

Benny nodded, and then Kate exclaimed, the light of excitement sparkling in her eyes.

"Yes! A dinner party. And let's have a rice table!"

She began to scribble notes, stopping to dart to store cupboards to check on various ingredients, and paused in the little cool side place where her father kept his modest stock of drinks. She came back to the table, frowning. "We seem to be terribly low on everything, Benny. I suppose Mummy wasn't feeling too good these last few weeks and didn't bother much."

She looked up at Benny, seeking confirmation that it was indeed so, and her mother had simply left the day-to-day routine to the houseboy.

He shook his head, and there was an awkwardness in the atmosphere which Kate sensed instantly. "Tuan said household accounts have to be kept down," he told her simply.

"Kept down?" she echoed. "I don't understand. Why, our store cupboards are like old Mother Hubbard's. I'm afraid you're going to have to go shopping, with a large list, if we're to have this dinner party."

Benny gave a shrug in which all the old fatalism of the East was expressed. Without speaking, he opened a drawer in the old-fashioned Dutch dresser and took out a battered old ledger. He held it out, and wordlessly Kate took it, to leaf through the pages.

She'd almost forgotten that anyone still kept household accounts these days. The past three years in her own flat in London had long since conditioned her to the hasty swanning through the supermarket to snatch up her weekly supply of convenience foods and a bottle of plonk, and the sketchy check on what she'd spent, when time permitted, before she stowed them away in her minute kitchenette. Now she looked over the recent entries in her father's hand, and saw the quantities on order gradually diminishing week by week. What on earth was her father playing at?

She closed the book with a snap. "Never mind, Benny, I'll talk to my father – he probably didn't realise, with my mother's sight being affected. Meanwhile, you'd better get down to the market."

She gave him some money and returned to the living room, her enthusiasm over the idea of a dinner party ebbing as quickly as it had arisen. Surely her father couldn't be starting an economy campaign. He was always talking about it, but that was as far as it got. All the inexplicable twinges of unease were back, and she was waiting impatiently for John Merrivale's return that evening.

Almost accusingly, she brandished the accounts book, and his laughter was the last reaction she had expected.

"What do you expect, Katy, from a mere man trying to keep the household budget balanced? Anyway, your mother and I live very simply when we're on our own, you know."

"Yes, but . . ." Kate stared at him, somehow not convinced. "I didn't realise until I had a check-up this morning."

"So you've been in the kitchen," he said sardonically. "I thought you were supposed to be on holiday – looking after your old parent in your spare time."

"I decided to give a dinner party, that's why," she said, ignoring his taunt.

"Why not?" He eyed her squarely. "Mahore isn't exactly a hive of entertainment, so we have to make our own. Better get it organised while you can still laugh at the same jokes."

"What do you mean?"

His shoulders lifted. "Exactly what I say. There are very few new faces here from one month to the next. Give it another couple of weeks, Katy, and you're going to be itching to get back to your swinging city." He smiled slightly. "I know! The term's already archaic by your standards."

"I wasn't going to say anything of the sort."

"No?" His whimsical smile came again. "Never mind. When are you plannning this at-home?"

"Next weekend. Sunday."

"Leave it till the following week. Walt may be away this coming weekend, and he'd be cut up if he missed it."

Kate's expression closed, and she turned away wordlessly. *Why* did everything always come back to Walt?

# CHAPTER THREE

SHE saw little of either Brad Sheridan or Walt during the following days, and as the uneventful week wore on, faithful to the tight little routine of the Mahore community, her father's words came back to her several times.

Already she was familiar with the pattern of the social round, and while she was still taken with the excitement of being home, amid all the remembered sights, smells, sounds and colour that made up the incomparable atmosphere of the East, she began to suspect that there might have been a ring of truth in her father's prophecy.

The routine, and the crowd, with one certain exception, were becoming rather predictable. The turn and return of invitation rarely varied, nor did the coffee mornings in the hot airless dimness behind shutters which kept out the sun but not the heat. The squash addicts rarely challenged the tennis clique, while the golf and fishing adherents remained faithful to their own, until all were reunited in the slaking of the evening thirst and the weekend jollifications at the club. The topics were shop, other people's wives and husbands, and the lamentable state of the rubber market.

One could lay a safe bet, Kate mused to herself, that Elaine and Rex would have at least one sulky wrangle during the week; that the Maddisons would cry off at least one engagement, ostensibly because Lena Maddison had a migraine, even while everyone knew that Tom Maddison was going to pieces again and his wife couldn't trust him not to disgrace her; and that Fay would introduce a new man, one of the new race of jet-borne executives who circled the international routes, living on their credit cards and out of their smart sleek air-weight luggage. Somehow it was always Fay who made acquaintance with the newcomers, who invariably checked in at the Mahore Majestic, and jerked them out of their jet-stress to introduce them briefly to Mahore society before they winged their way on to the next port of call.

"It's really pathetic," Elaine remarked on the Saturday evening as she watched the petite blonde widow drift by in the arms of a young American oil executive. "Why does she have to be so obvious? She'll be lying in wait for them at the airport before long!"

Kate's mouth compressed at the unconcealed bitchiness in the other girl's tone.

"I don't think so," she returned coolly. "After all, Fay's husband was P.R.O. for Mahore, and now she's P.A. to Lloyd, who took over, so it must be second nature to her to meet strangers."

"Second nature? You mean first, don't you?" Elaine sneered.

"*Ouch!* They're sharp tonight!" Walt edged in, nursing a lager in one pudgy fist. "Why not be honest, girlies? Fay's damned attractive. I'd pack up my drip-dry shirts for her any day."

"Who's stopping you?" Elaine's red lips curled.

"A certain unrequited yearning." Walt sighed and insinuated one arm around Kate's waist. "It goes back to my tender youth. They say one never quite forgets the girl next door. You didn't know that Kate used to be my girl next door, did you?"

Elaine raised finely plucked brows. "The touching reunion is somewhat belated, I'd say." She turned in search of the drink she had previously set down on a side table, and Kate seized the opportunity to free herself from Walt's unwelcome arm.

The movement brought her face to face with Brad Sheridan.

An electric bolt seemed to shoot home in her heart. She realised that the evening had been empty until this moment, and the thought stunned, even as he smiled and instantly set down his drink. Without speaking, he held open his arms and inclined his head towards the dance floor.

Silent herself, without even thought of resistance, she slipped into his arms and allowed him to guide her into the sluggishly moving circle of dancers. The night was heavy and close, and the features of the musicians up on the dais gleamed like wet teak. The air-conditioning seemed to be non-existent this

43

evening, and the big overhead fans seemed reluctant to spin, barely wafting the overheated air. But none of this occurred to Kate. She forgot the discomforting knowledge that the slightest effort on a night like this threatened to bring a film of moisture to her skin, and all the care in the world over make-up and grooming couldn't make her proof against the climate. A strange vivacity pervaded her body, and with it a certain satisfaction.

"I was beginning to think you've been avoiding me," Brad said at last, in unemotional tones.

"Avoiding you?" By now she was in full possession again of her normal outward poise, and her tones held just the right blend of surprise and coolness. "But why should I?"

"How should I know?" The slight movement of his shoulders communicated itself to her. "I haven't seen you since last weekend."

She controlled a small sigh. Sometimes she had wondered if she had imagined that strange conversation held with him on the night of the storm. Had he ever had that discussion he wanted with her father? There must have been several opportunities, yet neither had mentioned its taking place. Suddenly she longed to ask, to confide her own secret fears, without all the hedging and innuendo, so that she could dismiss this unease once and for all. But the barrier of restraint rose as strong and high as ever at the thought, and she pushed away the wistful desire.

"We were at the Maddisons' on Tuesday," she said quietly. "Fay was round on Wednesday. Walter took my father up to the lodge on Friday while I caught up on some domestic matters, and last night we stayed quietly at home. I could say that avoidance cuts two ways," she added coolly.

He ignored the delicate prompting behind this last remark, and asked: "Does your father often go up to that place?"

A tiny furrow came between Kate's silky brows. "I don't think so. Only for the occasional spot of fishing. Why?"

Again there was that subtle movement of his shoulders, and an answer that was a question. "Where exactly is this hideout of Marlow's?"

She looked up at him, surprised now. "To tell you the truth,

44

I don't know. I've never been there. He's only acquired it a couple of years ago, I believe."

"It's up the coast?"

She nodded. "Somewhere past Mas Telok. Well off the beaten track, I gather."

She waited, a little tense now, expecting further questions. But they did not come. Instead, Brad looked down into her questioning eyes and imperceptibly steered her towards the edge of the floor, to a point where wide patio doors opened on to the terrace. The music muted as she passed with Brad into the dark scented warmth of the night. Painted parchment lanterns cast soft pools and streaks of luminescence across the garden, and clouds of moths made shadowy amber haloes which whirred ceaselessly round the lamps. In a secluded arbour Brad stopped.

Kate's heart quickened, but with the quickening came wariness. He seemed to have forgotten his interest in Walt's hideaway, and instinct provided a more obvious answer. She looked up at the tall shadowy figure, and with a small pang of regret decided it might be wiser to correct any impression that she was now prepared to indulge in a resumption of last week's more amorous exchange. For her own peace of mind she had to write that off as an isolated incident, not to be repeated ... She moved on a slow pace, pretending fascination as she gently touched the delicate white beauty of a blossom that had opened great waxy petals to the night.

Brad watched the slender caressing fingers and murmured: "One night of fulfilment."

"What?"

"The moonflower."

"Oh, yes ..." Kate looked at the night blossom whose perfection was so pitifully brief, as was so much of the wild and beautiful fecundity of tropical life. A tiny shiver touched her and Brad put his hand on her arm.

"Cold?"

"Here?" she laughed. "You can't be serious!"

He shrugged and fell into step with her as she moved on along the twisting path under the lamplit trees. "What are you doing tomorrow?"

"I don't know." She stared up at the bland face of the moon, tonight unclouded. "Go out in the boat, maybe."

"With your father?"

"If he wants to." She blew gently at an insect fluttering near her face. "It depends."

"Spend the day with me."

She turned. "The whole day?"

He nodded. "I'm free all day. We'll plan it as it comes."

Suddenly she felt a wild elation, and cast all doubts aside. She smiled. "All right! I'd love to."

"Good. Straight after breakfast too early?"

"Depends what time you have breakfast."

His teeth glimmered whitely. "I doubt if you'd be rubbing the sleep out of those challenging eyes by then, sweet Kate. Shall we say eight? – and you'd better be on the doorstep."

"Eight! The morning's past its best by then."

He slipped one arm round her waist and began to walk her back towards the lights of the terrace. "Maybe we'd better make a start now," he said softly.

"Maybe we'd better not," she returned calmly, for once conceding that he'd had the last word, and for once not caring a scrap.

She found she was looking forward with increasing pleasure to the outing, and, just before they left the club that evening, she admitted a purely vindictive delight into her heart when Walt invited himself over to the Merrivales' for the following day and she kept a discreet silence about her own plans until she and her father reached home. She certainly didn't anticipate any objections – hadn't her father insisted she treat her stay as an extended holiday, and hadn't he expressed concern at her apparent indifference to some invitations received? So she was somewhat surprised at the troubled look which settled on his face when she told of the arrangement she had made.

"I wish you'd told me," he sighed. "I'd have put Walt off."

"It isn't too late to do that." She met her father's gaze with a direct steadiness and saw his glance waver away. "After all, he invited himself. Ring him now. He'll not have had time to turn in."

John Merrivale shook his head. "No, let it stand. But I wish you'd spoken out at the time, Katy."

"But why? I didn't want to." Her lips closed firmly. "It would have meant broadcasting my affairs to the entire club tonight. You know what they are."

He nodded. For a moment he was silent, and with a sickening flash of dismay she thought he was both angry and frightened. Then he swung round abruptly.

"Kate, you're not having an affair with Brad Sheridan, are you?"

"Me? With Brad?" Her eyes glinted with relief and a certain ironic amusement. "Good heavens, no. He simply asked me out for a drive, that's all. But even if I were, it's no concern of anyone else."

"I know." John Merrivale passed one hand over his silvering hair. "But I'd got the impression you didn't like Sheridan."

Kate looked back at him reflectively, some deep-set instinct warning her to choose her words with care. "Maybe I did give you that impression, but it isn't strictly true. Let's say that I was wary of him – still am – because I felt that something was bothering you and that in some way Brad was involved. But as you insist that there's nothing to get steamed up over I can only conclude that I was imagining things."

She waited for the assurance of ready confirmation that would finally set her mind at rest, but it did not come. Something almost like a spasm of pain passed over her father's features, and an incredulous fear flashed into her mind.

"Father . . ." she took a step forward, "he – he's not married, or something?"

"What?" He seemed surprised, as though this was the last objection that would occur to him. The small laugh he gave struck Kate as forced. "No, not as far as I know. I'd say he was too crafty to get caught in the silken snare. No, Katy, it's not that. I – I was just a bit surprised, that's all."

Kate studied him with worried eyes. For the first time she considered more dispassionately the alacrity with which she had accepted Brad's invitation, and the even stranger elation that even now was bubbling up within her, just at the thought of spending a day with him. Reluctantly she suppressed the tremor of excitement and said slowly:

"Do you really mind? Because if so, I could cry off. If you want me to stay home and play hostess I will." She fought down the stab of disappointment that came with her offer and waited anxiously for his reply.

It came almost brusquely, with a heartiness that lacked conviction. "No, I wouldn't hear of it. Forget it, Katy. Go and enjoy yourself." He yawned, stretched his arms high and sagged. "I don't know about *you*, but I'm for bed."

"Just a moment ..." she put out her hand, "sure you're not angry with me?"

"Oh, Katy!" He came to her and cupped her face between his palms. "I'm sorry. But I just can't get used to the idea of you making your own decisions about people and things. You've become so independent these last few years. Sometimes I can't believe it." He sighed, and his hands dropped away.

"Believe what? That I'm any different inside?" she asked softly, moved by the emotion glimpsed in his face. "I'm not really, you know."

He nodded. "The trouble is, darling, as one gets older life seems to pass so much more quickly, but inside one tends still to see things and people as they were. Somehow I still expect the young, exuberant Katy to rush to me with that coaxing look in her eyes and a demand for permission to do something, or go somewhere," he gestured, "and looking at me all the time as though I might refuse to grant her the paradise in a child's whim. You'll have to give me time to get used to the fact that she's grown up and gained the authority of managing her own life for five long years."

"Oh, Daddy!" The old childish endearment slipped out as she threw her arms round him. "I haven't changed as much as that. You've been a brooding old bear, haven't you?"

"Not really." He gave her a tight hug, then released her. "Put it down to the onset of old age. And Walt and I will drown our sorrows down at Nick's. I won't breathe a word about you – when I think about it, I'm not sure I want to encourage Walt, or Brad, or anyone else, to lay siege to my daughter's hand. So keep your heart, lass, do you hear?"

"I'll try."

Reassured, she dropped a kiss on his cheek and bade him goodnight, then began her preparations for the morning. Of course she would heed her father's advice – but one couldn't refuse all male invitations lest one lost one's heart in the process. So why shouldn't she enjoy a mild flirtation with Brad Sheridan? As long as it was played on *her* terms.

Singing a soft little melody under her breath she deliberated over her choice of dress for the next day. A flash of pride insisted that she must appear at her coolest, most flawlessly groomed best. Not that the climate would allow her to remain like that for very long! Unless she took along several changes of clothing and a portable shower! But there was no reason why the first impression should not dazzle.

She slept lightly and sweetly that night, and was astir before the dawn. She made a sparing breakfast, just iced papaya and a crispbread, then took her shower and dressed. She was putting the finishing touches to her make-up and applying iced perfume stick to her temples when Benny brought the note.

She knew before she opened it what it would contain.

*"Called away. Forgive me until I make my apologies in person.*
*B.S."*

Not a word of explanation. She crumpled the note and looked round as her father came to the open doorway. She shook her head wordlessly and tossed the crumpled ball of paper into the waste-paper bin.

\*     \*     \*

In the mood she was in, it was not easy to be pleasantly sociable with Walt, but for her father's sake Kate did her best. Walt arrived about eleven, they had drinks, an early lunch, and then settled down to endure those enervating midday hours when every movement seemed an effort in the airless heat.

After what she deemed a polite interval Kate excused herself and went to shower and change. Almost deliberately, she donned an old pair of faded blue cotton flares which were not only somewhat obsolete fashionwise but were positively threadbare.

49

But they were cool and comfortable, and needed only a loose cotton shirt, carelessly slicked hair and a face devoid of any make-up to complete the off-camera-duty Kate which only the privacy of her flat and a few close friends ever saw. She eyed her reflection almost defiantly. To her own self-critical scrutiny she looked untidy, ill-groomed and half-dressed, but it was the only way she knew to kill a certain traitorous hope that had persisted all morning: that the day might yet bring a note, or even Brad himself, to say that the day might yet be theirs.

With a scornful little grimace for sentimental naivete Kate left her room and went with reluctant steps to rejoin her father and Walt. But they were both asleep, sprawled on the loungers in the shade of the patio. Walt's sand-coloured hair had fallen over his brow, his mouth had gone slack, and in the relaxation of sleep too much spare flesh bulged under his sweat-patched shirt. Kate's mouth curled downwards at the corner; he was not exactly a prepossessing sight. They talked about women letting themselves go, but Walt was certainly a classic male case. If he took a little more exercise, a little less food and alcohol . . . Her glance strayed to the fallen line of the bottle of Bols which her father had opened that morning and her mouth tightened again. Without any sound she turned away, to return to her room, where she drew the shades and flopped down on her bed after switching on the cooling fan.

Kate slept longer than she had intended, and the next thing she knew was Benny awakening her with a cup of tea and telling her it was four-thirty. To her relief Walt had gone, and she found her father alone in the sitting room. But her relief was shortlived when he told her they were eating at the club that evening with Walt.

"Count me out," she said flatly, picking up her book and subsiding into a chair.

John Merrivale looked at his daughter's morose expression and said with unwonted sharpness: "Why? It's better than mooning around here because you've been stood up for the day. I thought you had more pride, Kate."

She stared at him over the top of the book. The attack seemed unfair as well as unexpected. "I don't see what pride has to do with avoiding an invitation I neither wanted nor accepted, Father."

He sighed. "You make a simple invitation to dine sound like a penance."

"It is in this case."

Unfamiliar anger tightened his face. "By that I take it you aren't coming?"

"That's right." She stared stubbornly at her book, refusing to admit her father's annoyance. "Haven't we had enough of Walt Marlow for one day?"

A heavy sigh made John Merrivale's shoulders sag. "I wish you'd try to make things easier, Kate. They're difficult enough already without . . ."

"Without what? I don't understand." She laid the book aside, aware of tension in the atmosphere again. "Father, I know Uncle Matt was your dearest friend, but I've no intention of allowing his son to become mine. It's as simple as that."

"That's an exaggeration." John Merrivale groped for his cigarettes and lit one with a hand that moved jerkily. "In a matter of weeks you'll be leaving again. Is it so much to ask that you try to hide your dislike of Walt for that short time? I thought you, of all people, understood what it's like living in a tight community like this. You can't escape working colleagues in a place like this. And I have to go on working with these people when you've gone. We have to keep personal relationships reasonably smooth or work becomes hell."

He fell silent, then turned away with a shrug. "But you must please yourself. I suppose we must all seem pretty provincial company after the set you mix with in London."

"It isn't that at all!" Kate sat up sharply. "Sometimes I get the impression you're almost frightened of Walt Marlow."

"What?" He swung round so abruptly she was surprised. "Kate, what nonsense you talk! Now why should I be frightened of Walt?"

"That's what I'm asking you." She stared at him, almost sure she detected unease, if not actual fear, behind the expression of amazement he had assumed. It was forced, she was positive, and the chill crept round her heart again. "Why do you seem to try to protect Walt, pander to him, all the time?"

"I don't, Kate." He shook his head, control back over the brief lapse from his usual placid demeanour. "You're not the only one to have suffered an ill-crossed affair of the heart, you know."

"Don't tell me Walt's been crossed in love." Her mouth twisted with cynicism. "My heart bleeds at the thought."

"It's true. But actually it was just as well the affair came to grief. She was an expensive piece," John said reflectively, perhaps forgetting he was talking to his daughter instead of another man. "She dropped Walt like a hot cake and transferred her favours to one of the engineers down at the refinery. The days when rubber could compete with oil are over," he added dryly.

"Well, don't expect me to do any consoling," Kate said flatly.

"I don't." John sighed again and rubbed at his chin. "I suppose I'd better go and shave."

The stoop of his shoulders betrayed defeat as he moved away, and suddenly Kate forgot her pique. Impulsively she got to her feet and ran to him. "I'm sorry – that was all rather petty of me. And don't ever say I find you dull. You know how much I love you, dearest Father."

"I know." Instantly he put a gentle arm around her shoulders. "The blame's mine. Of course you must choose your friends as you wish while you're here. But I thought ..."

"Yes?" she prompted.

"Nothing, just that I hate to see you hurt, Katy."

"But I'm not hurt! Can't we have honest arguments now and again?"

"I didn't mean that." His eyes searched her face. "I mean the spoiled day."

"Oh, that ..." she injected scorn into her voice. "I'm not hurt over that!"

"Perhaps not." His glance was shrewd. "But you were very disappointed, weren't you?"

"What girl wouldn't?" Kate gave a rueful smile. "After all the style I put on, only to be left as flat as the proverbial pancake. But never mind," she reached up to hug him, "I'll put it all on again for tonight. Okay?"

"That's my girl,"

He returned her hug, but she knew she had not imagined the rush of relief in his eyes as he realised she had changed her mind about accompanying him that evening.

True to her promise, she took more than special care over getting ready for the evening and tried to ignore the taunting knowledge that there was no joy in that special care, or in the cool, attractive girl who met her gaze through the mirror as she prepared to leave.

All the same tormenting questions were back. What was troubling her father? For he would never have shown anger as he had done tonight, not over a purely personal decision like today's. For even as a child she had been allowed freedom of choice in many ways, as long as her father foresaw no harm which might result. True, he might have tried to jolly her into something she did not want to do, or shown impatience, but never anger. So why was it so important to him that she be nice to Walt? Kate's thoughts checked at the words they had chosen, and their other unpleasant if old-fashioned implication. She was being quite ridiculous and childish, she decided with a swift change of mood. It was natural that he would be annoyed after making the arrangement on her behalf. And after all, didn't she have to be very pleasant to certain photographers, buyers, and other people she sometimes had to work with in the course of her job? Didn't she often thank her lucky stars she had become successful enough to have some choice in her assignments? Because in her job she met some men – and women – with very strange ideas on having fun.

Kate stepped back and switched off the wall light. Why didn't she face the truth? She was disappointed over the day's failure to bring Brad Sheridan. Her father had been quite right – she was hurt. Surely Brad could have added a few more words of explanation.

Kate fought down the hurt to her pride from merely admitting that small truth and went to join her father.

*

It was a lovely evening, one of those warm tropic nights beloved of romantic movies but not always so perfect in reality. Now that it was dark Mahore seethed with life. Lanterns made bright splashes of coloured radiance above the pavement cafés where music blared and varied smells of oriental fare floated forth. Chinese, Indians, Malays, Tamils, old and young, thronged the sidewalks. Slim-hipped boys sporting gay shirts idled in groups, slender graceful girls in their best dresses giggled among themselves even as they moved with the sinuous flowing walk of the East, trishaws shot and weaved in death-defying spurts among the horn-blasting cars, and from the arcades touted invitations to sample joys dubious or otherwise merged with the flaring hiss of the acetylene lamps. On the other side of the road the river gleamed sluggishly, the moored boats and sampans hung with lights that mingled with the reflections on the water.

The club lay on the far side of town, just out of hearing distance from the open-air dance hall and the big amusement park. Kate looked at the fairy-light hoop that spanned the entrance and remembered how she had always yearned to sample its excitement. But all during her childhood it had been taboo as far as she was concerned, unless accompanied by an adult, which of course took all the sense of adventure away. As the lights fell away into the darkness behind the speeding car she thought of Brad Sheridan; he would be the ideal companion for that venture into Eastern delight.

By the time Walt drove the car into a parking space she had regained her humour and decided that her view on life had been remarkably unreasonable that day. It must be the atmosphere of the East that was making her suspicions work overtime and her senses too sensitive. In a while she would probably look back and wonder why on earth she'd worried.

Walt locked the car and took her arm as they walked towards the entrance. Kate made no move to disengage herself, and, still imbued with her new philosophy of accepting human nature with all its foibles, laughed at the trite joke he made as Tom and Lena appeared from the opposite side of the car park. The meeting brought the usual flurry of small-talk greetings and the formation of a group on the shallow flight of steps

54

leading up to the doorway. Kate did not notice the couple emerging from the entrance, until Walt took her arm again to draw her aside and murmured softly, "Ho, ho, what have we here?" in a meaning voice.

Kate moved to make way, turning as she did so, and the smile fled from her lips. The couple leaving were Brad Sheridan and Elaine Winton.

Elaine's eyes were bright and her laughter brittle. She was clinging to Brad as though she owned him, and he seemed unaware of anything untoward in his arm wrapped closely round Elaine's slender waist. "Darling, let's go somewhere different," she was saying. "I want to – " Her bright gaze encompassed the newcomers, and something of Kate's shocked expression must have struck her. Her smile faltered for a moment, then flashed triumphantly. "You don't mind, do you? I've only borrowed him while Rex is away." Her glance roved the others in the circle of faces. "Rex is always leaving me. Shocking, isn't it?"

Kate looked at Brad, as though she doubted the evidence of her own eyes. He stared back at her, his expression unreadable, and hesitated. For a moment she thought he was going to speak, then Elaine said impatiently: "Come on, darling. You can see they don't approve of us."

Kate saw the tightening line of his mouth and felt a cold sickness gather in her stomach. With an effort she forced a smile. "Why should I mind, Elaine? Have a good time – both of you."

She averted her face and walked through the swing doors, her head held high and her features under cold control. She heard the murmurs of conjecture among Tom and Lena and Walt, and wished with all her heart she had followed her earlier inclination and stayed at home. That way she would at least have been spared the sight she had just witnessed. Brad and Elaine Winton. . . . All her initial instincts had been accurate. Girls were all the same for Brad Sheridan. He took them as they came, married or not. Kate tried to stifle her disillusion and went into the dining room.

If only the evening were over. The meal tasted like sawdust and the wine like vinegar, and the chatter round her was like voices dimly perceived beyond a glass barrier. Afterwards she danced, with Walt, with Tom, with Lloyd, and downed three gin slings before her father suddenly asked: "Are you all right, Katy?"

"Me? Of course I'm all right, I'm fine!" She held out her hand. "Come on, I'll wake you up on the dance floor to prove it."

But three dances and another gin sling later she realised that she wasn't all right. She had a splitting headache and she felt slightly sick. She went in search of her father, who by now was ensconced in the card lounge, and told him she was going home.

He put down his hand and stood up. "No, we'll both go, Katy."

She looked at his concerned expression and shook her head, knowing how much he enjoyed a game of solo with three friends of his own generation. "I'll get a taxi. I'm not going to spoil your game."

"I'll take Kate home."

Walt had followed her and she sighed wearily, knowing she could not refuse.

"Sure you'll be okay?" John Merrivale said doubtfully, obviously torn between duty and desire to finish the game.

"Sure." She kissed him lightly. "I'm just going to fall into bed with a couple of aspirins. I'll be fine by morning."

Walt was particularly solicitous, holding her wrap, helping her into the car, and turning off the stereo cassette player. She settled back, her hand to her throbbing temples, and the car had covered some distance before she realised that he had taken the coast road turning as they left the town.

She started up, peering through the glass, and Walt said soothingly: "You've got a headache, so I thought the night air and the darkness might help. Why don't you close your eyes and relax?"

It seemed unusually thoughtful for Walt. She watched his pale hand reach to adjust the flow from the air-conditioner, then return to the wheel before she tried to dismiss unease and do as he advised. It was quite true; the dark road up the coast would be quiet and restful after the bright noise of the club's atmosphere. Maybe a short drive would do the trick.

The coast road climbed steadily, narrowing and leaving the coastline at one point to skirt a plantation, until the long dark avenue of silent sentinels gave way to a wilder terrain and the uncultivated mass of jungle that rose like a wall about to topple across the narrow track. And then the track dropped again, nearing the sea and traversing a rough suspension bridge that spanned the Taikiang Delta. By daylight it was quite an awe-inspiring drive, but by night it was eerie. A great brooding melon moon was rising, casting strange shadows, and Kate experienced fresh unease. Surely Walt didn't intend driving right up to Mas Telok?

She remembered his place up there, and her mouth twisted wryly. Was this his intended destination? She prayed not; an amorous Walt was the last prospect she felt like contending with at the moment. She turned her head, to ask the question, and as she moved she felt the car's speed lessen. There was a series of bumps, the protest of tyres, and a jolt as Walt applied the handbrake. They were off the road, in what seemed to be a clearing, and a moon-bathed sea glittered into the distance.

"Where on earth are we?" Kate found her voice and hoped it sounded casual. "Don't tell me you've run out of juice!"

"I'm not as careless as that." Walt switched off the engine. "Don't you know where we are?"

"No. Should I?"

"Yes." Walt killed the headlights and the moon's glow resolved into its own mystic ambience. He looked at her, and something in his heavy features made her breath still.

She drew her light stole closer round her shoulders. "It – it must be getting late. Hadn't we better turn back?"

"We've just got here. Let's look at the sea."

Kate bit her lip, about to protest, then decided she had better humour him. Slowly she got out of the car and walked across the clearing. From the edge the ground fell away steeply to a rocky shore below, now a lunar landscape of great black and silver hollows. And suddenly Kate remembered.

A cold tremor ran through her body. This could only be ... This was the headland of P'bhamg Batee. She gave a small gasp and turned to run, but Walt's hand shot out to encircle her arm.

"I wonder if it's still there," he said tonelessly.

"If — if what is still there?" Kate's lips felt stiff.

"You know what I'm talking about. Why pretend?"

The cold shivers began to chase down Kate's spine again. What had possessed Walt to revisit the scene of the old tragedy? What morbid impulse had made him drive her here, to stand on this volcanic ledge and surmise on the fate of the car in which Leila Denton had driven to her death all those years ago?

At last she whispered: "I'm not pretending, Walt. I'm sorry, believe me. But what good will all this do?" She gave a helpless gesture and stared unseeingly across the moonlit void of the Strait.

There was an ominous silence from the man at her side, and when she could bear it no longer she swung to face him. "Let's go back now, please. It's getting terribly late."

He turned then, savagely. "It's always the same with you, Kate. You don't want to know."

She recoiled. "I don't understand. What do you mean? I don't want to know?"

"I mean this." He seized her by the shoulders. "You've deliberately avoided me ever since you got here. Yes, you have. It was the same five years ago, when you came home from that snobby boarding school in England and I asked you out for a meal. It was the same years ago. Even as a child you used to avoid me like the plague."

The attack stunned her into silence. It was so appallingly near the truth she could summon little defence. Had she shown her dislike so blatantly? But what else did one do to stifle unwanted attentions when the other party persisted in ignoring the usual accepted social excuses and evasions? Certainly she had never, to the best of her knowledge, been rude or betrayed that dislike she couldn't repress even when she tried. She had always been polite, but fear of seeming to give encouragement had kept her manner cool. Now it seemed Walt had always perceived the truth. Oh, God, she thought desperately. What can I say?

"I'm sure you can't hold my childhood actions against me,"

she said helplessly. "There's almost ten years between us, Walt. What could a small child have in common with a teenage boy?" Her shoulders lifted and fell resignedly. "I never intended to – to give offence, not deliberately."

"Didn't you?" His voice roughened. "But you can give your favours to a stranger, to a trouble-making newcomer who hasn't been here five minutes."

"That's not true!" The darkness helped to disguise the hot colour that flowed into her cheeks. For there could be no doubt as to whom he referred. "And even if I did it's no concern of anyone, except myself."

Walt ignored this, his fingers cutting into the soft flesh of her upper arms. "You didn't have a headache tonight. That was an excuse. Because you couldn't bear to be passed over in favour of another woman. How do you think it feels to be treated like that all the time? Every time you suggest a date, to be put off with cold excuses? To be looked at as though you hardly existed? The way you've treated me."

"I didn't know!" she cried wildly, trying to free herself. "How could I? I didn't know!" she repeated.

"That I wanted you?" he said between clenched teeth. "I've always wanted you. But you didn't want to know." Suddenly he dragged her against him and forced his mouth on her startled lips.

The hot pressure of Walt's sensual mouth made Kate go rigid with shock for a moment. Then revulsion sparked fierce life into her limbs. She lashed out, scarcely knowing what she was doing in her frantic effort to break free. Her flailing fist caught him on his eye and his head jerked back.

"You wildcat! You – "

"You asked for that!" With a violent twist Kate was free. "How dare you? You brought me here deliberately. Did you really expect me to fall into your arms? Did you – "

"Don't play the innocent. You of all poeple, Kate." His mouth twisted into an ugly sneer. "Or you'll regret it."

Kate took a step back. She took a hunted glance about her.

"Are you threatening me?" she gasped.

"I'm warning you."

"Warning me? But what ..."

Kate took a step back. Walt must be drunk, or off balance. What did he mean? She threw a hunted glance round her, fear closing in as the full implication of her plight began to hit home. They were miles from anywhere. Even if she turned to run there was nowhere to go. She couldn't possibly *walk* back from here. She put out a placatory hand.

"Walt, listen ... I don't know what I'm supposed to have said, or done, but please ... can't we discuss it somewhere else? Let's go back, and – and have a drink, and – " She bit her lip, staring up at his vindictive face. "My father will be home by now – he'll be worrying."

"Your father!"

The derision in the exclamation drove the colour from Kate's cheeks. Walt gave a scornful laugh. "I often think it's a good job for you that I was a discreet little boy," he sneered.

"What do you mean?" Kate's hand went to her mouth. "What *is* all this?"

"Still pretending you don't know?" The moonlight glimmered on Walt's ugly smile. "Oh, Kate, stop taking me for a fool."

"I've never taken you for that." Kate turned away and pressed pale fingers against her face. Suddenly she knew that Walt was neither crazed nor drunk, and that he had brought her here for a special reason. She also knew, with a flash of blind instinct, that this vengeful anger was in some way connected with her father's disturbed mein of late. Her hands fell slowly to her sides. "I think you'd better tell me exactly what all these insinuations mean," she said quietly.

"I mean that *your* father was responsible for my stepmother's death."

There was a dreadful silence. Kate stood frozen with shock. The words did not register properly, did not make sense. Her father. Leila Denton. Why did people still think of her as Leila Denton instead of Mrs. Marlow? The silence became a roaring in Kate's ears, then resolved into the sound of the sea. She whirled round.

"You must be out of your mind!"

"Is that all you can say? It's true!" He thrust his face near, compelling her horrified gaze. "It's true, and nothing will make it otherwise. Your father was the man."

Kate recoiled. "I don't believe it. I can't!" Desperately she watched Walt shake his head mockingly. Desperately she sought for means to refute the monstrous accusation. "How? Why – if there's anything – why was nothing said at the time? Why wasn't there any – any inquiry, any ...?" Her voice faltered and broke. "I don't believe it," she repeated. "How can you say such a – such an appalling thing?"

"Because I heard it all."

"You?" Her mouth gaped with disbelief. "You heard – *what?*"

"My stepmother was crazy over him. She only married my father to get away from the mess her life was. Then she met your father, and he didn't need much encouragement. Oh, they thought no one knew." Walt's mouth twisted. "But I knew all right."

Kate took a deep sobbing breath. But before she could protest Walt rushed on, as though some long-dammed spate was suddenly released.

"They used to meet down in Mahore, at the Colonial. And at the lagoon beach. And once I saw them up at the Kalung sector. She was supposed to be going to the Maddisons, but she didn't. She went to the sector because your father was due up there that day. I know because I followed her. And that's when they decided to go away together."

Kate shook her head unbelievingly. She wanted to blot out everything she was hearing, all those dreadful, damning statements concerning her beloved father. She gave a strangled little murmur, and Walt nodded, almost as though with satisfaction.

"I really believe you didn't know," he said mockingly, "but I suppose it's not really surprising. After all, who would tell you? Not *my* father, for although he suspected there was another man in Leila's life, he never suspected his closest friend. And I can't imagine *your* father telling you, not the man you idolise. The man I've always been expected to look up to," Walt sneered. "And even then he didn't have the guts to follow through. He turned scared. Leila waited two days for him to go to her. She had the tickets in her bag for both of them, all ready. But he never turned up. By then it was too late. She couldn't go back – she'd be too scared by then. So she put an end to it altogether. The only way she had left."

A shuddering sigh escaped Kate's bloodless lips. All the garbled little bits of gossip, supposition, came flooding back into her memory. That there had been another man. That somehow that had gone wrong. And Leila, in the dreadful moment of final despair, had taken her life.

"Yes," said Walt. "Your father was responsible, as sure as if he'd been at the wheel of that car."

"Oh no!" Kate moaned softly. "I can't believe it. Not – not my father."

Walt nodded. "I've proof. The notes I found afterwards, among her things. My father was too upset to go through her papers – not that she had much. I had to do that."

Kate stared at the moonlit sea, but saw only the ugliness of the past superimposed upon the loveliness. Something in her heart told her that the ring of truth echoed throughout his words. It took little imagination to picture the adolescent Walt snooping and watching, sneaking out after the unsuspecting Leila, listening, going through her personal bits and pieces afterwards . . . pocketing the pathetic scraps of proof. But no matter how damning it might seem Kate would never believe that her father had been so totally unfaithful. Foolish perhaps, but never . . .

Tears misted Kate's eyes. Had her mother ever guessed? Had she known? A surge of pure hatred swelled in Kate's heart. How dared Walt drag it all up again? And how could she stand here, accepting his cruel allegations? She had only his word, and for all she knew the whole thing could be a string of spiteful lies. But why . . .?

"I never told anyone," Walt said, as though divining the trend of her thoughts. "Nobody else ever knew."

"Then why have you told me? Why suddenly bring up a tragedy that's fifteen years old? Not that I'm convinced," she flashed.

"I could convince you, if necessary."

There was quiet deadliness in his tone. His former bluster and accusatory force had vanished, but this new quietness was infinitely more menacing, and convincing.

Kate thought of her father, instinct telling her to deny and challenge, until she heard the truth from her father's lips. She whispered, "But what good would it do? What does it matter whether I believe you or not? It won't change anything now."

"That's why I'm telling you. Because I don't want anything to change." Abruptly Walt turned away, grasping her arm and beginning to walk towards the car.

Dazedly she moved with automatic steps, bewilderment succeeding the initial shock of the revelation she had just heard. When they reached the car she stopped and licked dry lips. She stared up at him. "Why, Walt? I must know. What do you want from me?"

He opened the car door. "Do I actually detect a slight change in the lady's tone?"

The cruel twist on his mouth sent a shiver through Kate. She said raggedly: "I might have known – immoral blackmail."

He laughed unpleasantly. "Nothing so dramatic – I'm not such a fool as to expect such ready accommodation from you, my dear Kate."

"What else am I to imagine? But I'm not going to be blackmailed by you, Walt, either immorally or otherwise."

He shrugged. "You have little choice, I'm afraid. But if you're wise you'll remember this."

Kate tensed. Here it was; the reckoning. "Well," she said through bloodless lips, "what's your price?"

"I can be a good friend – or a bad enemy. If you value your father's happiness you'll remember this in future. And there's one other thing . . ."

Kate's nails were cutting into her palms as she faced him. She waited wordlessly, and the brilliant moonlight lit the bitter sneer on Walt's mouth.

"Keep away from Brad Sheridan. If you don't you'll regret it."

# CHAPTER FOUR

THERE was little sleep for Kate that night.

All through the dark hours she tossed and turned restlessly, imprisoned with the full reality of shock and horror under the stifling confine of her mosquito net.

It couldn't be true. Not her father – and Leila Denton.

Every instinct had urged her to confront her father, to beg his denial, to implore him to tell her it was all a hideous lie.

But she couldn't. Her courage quailed and she crept into bed, despising her craven self as she lay silent and listened to the sounds of her father's return. When he opened her door and said softly: "All right, girl?" she made no reply, forcing her breathing to come lightly and evenly until he withdrew and gently closed the door. How could she challenge him? Probe into a fifteen-year-old tragedy, to ask: *Did you betray my mother and your best friend? Did you cause the death of the other woman who loved you?*

It can't be true, Kate repeated desperately to herself, over and over again. She would never believe it. But Walt said he had proof. *What proof?* And did this mean ...?

Kate stared into the darkness, forcing herself to be calm. She must find out the truth, no matter how much it might hurt. If she didn't she would never know peace of mind again. Despite the clammy heat of the night she grew chilled as she faced the damning possibilities that could add up to the truth she feared. All those small, isolated doubts, her mother's unease and dimly sensed knowledge that all was not well, the little things, which, taken separately could be logically explained, but put together ... Had Walt been blackmailing her father all these years?

Kate huddled beneath the single covering, and her lips set in a bloodless line. No wonder her beloved father had looked so drawn and weary at times. And as for Walt ... A surge of pure hatred set the adrenalin coursing in her veins until she was trembling and clenching her fists till they hurt. Whichever way one looked at it, it was sheer blackmail – moral as far as she was concerned, and heaven knew what for her father. When Walt had set her down at the bungalow there had been no mistaking the meaning in his eyes. He had denied it verbally, but Kate had no illusions.

For long shivering moments she had thought he was about to start pawing her again, but to her eternal thankfulness he changed his mind. Perhaps it had penetrated even his selfish skin that any goodnight adieus of that nature were impossible in Kate's present mood. She could still hear his voice, hear him say, as though nothing had happened: "I'll see you tomorrow, about seven, here. Okay?"

What else could she do but agree? When every instinct warned of the danger in refusing.

Kate was wan and dull-eyed when she dragged herself up to face the new day. Her father watched with concerned eyes as she picked at her breakfast and finally pushed her plate aside almost untouched. When she poured a cup of black coffee and lit a cigarette John Merrivale frowned.

"Those aren't much good as a pick-me-up, Katy. Try and eat something."

"I'm not hungry." She sipped listlessly at her coffee. "I'll be okay when I've had a breath of air."

"Air!" Her father ran his hand round the neck of his shirt. "You say that as though you were about to step out into an English country garden in spring. It's stifling outside!"

The thought invoked a semi-hysterical reaction. She shook her head, and he gave her another anxious look. "You're dreadfully pale. What's wrong, Kate?"

She wanted to scream: Everything! With an effort she controlled herself and forced a smile. "Can't you see that your daughter has a hangover and feels very ashamed of herself?"

"I hope that's all it is." John Merrivale stood up and paused beside Kate's chair. "Take things easy today, darling." He touched her cheek. "Why not go back to bed?"

"I may do that." She upturned a pale face for his kiss and sat unmoving until he had gone from the house. When the sound of the car faded she sighed and poured out a second cup of coffee.

What was she going to do?

Tackle her father and demand the truth? That was the only way to get the answers she needed to deal with the matter. Because she couldn't allow it to go on. If Walt was using the foul power of blackmail he had to be stopped. But how to keep it all from her mother?

Kate pressed a hand to her aching head. There seemed no way out that wouldn't bring disaster. She remembered the unexpected parsimony she had discovered the day she checked the store cupboards, and Benny's disclosure about her father's insistence that the household accounts must be kept down. And there was this impression all the time of a pandering to Walt's desires. Even the impression that her father wished her to maintain as friendly a relationship as possible with Walt, and his remarks a few days ago that now seemed to have a deeper significance: that in a few weeks she would be out of it all again, far away, while he would still be there ...

Kate got up and wandered restlessly round the house, looking into every room with the discerning eye of worry. Certainly there were traces of shabbiness here and there, and the inevitable effects of a climate that took its toll of so many things. Anything originally from nature was vulnerable. Timbers rotted, fibres wilted under the onslaught of the mould and mildew that insinuated grey spores into every receptive surface. Making allowances for the constant battle against these tropical ravages the house was still a comfortable, adequate home, if not exactly a luxurious one. Kate's parents were not by nature discontented, always in pursuit of the latest luxury or the newest gimmick. Their possessions were well chosen, to be serviceable and comfortable, and of necessity, most of the furniture was cane, but Mrs. Merrivale's quiet good taste was evident everywhere in the cool simplicity of her pastel colour schemes. Ice blues and cloud-pale greens predominated in both wall decor and soft furnishings, and stronger contrasts were kept to a minimum – outside, the great tropical earth mother provided ample gaudy and exotic colour all around the small oasis of cool tranquillity that was home.

Kate sighed. No, there was nothing seriously to suggest a drain in finance, except the one matter of the kitchen accounts. And when she had jokingly challenged her father about that he had simply told her to get what she wanted for her dinner party. He had also reminded her that it was common practice for Benny to go to market early each morning to buy the day's supply of perishable goods. Which Kate had to admit was true. And after all, it was possible that he'd had an impulsive notion to prove to his wife when she returned that he had not been inordinately extravagant during her absence.

If only she could convince herself that it wasn't money. Kate went to her mother's dressing table, opening the Chinese lacquer cabinet which in its nest of tiny drawers and compartments held her mother's personal treasures.

They were all there still: the gold watch, old-fashioned now, that had been her bridal gift from her husband, the double rope of milky pearls in which Kate could remember entwining small fingers many years ago, the jade ring, and the amethyst pendent lying there among the silver wriggles of its chain. Yes, they were all there, the pretty things Kate could recall, with two exceptions, the engagement ring and a silver filigree brooch which Mrs. Merrivale had probably worn when she set out on her long journey to England.

Kate closed the little drawers and returned to the lounge, her eyes purposeful now. Much as her sensibilities recoiled in disgust she had to go on. She went to the bureau and opened the left-hand drawer. Her father might be carrying his cheque book, but he usually kept the old ones for some time, at least until the end of each financial year.

She found two of them straight away. Hating herself for prying but knowing she had to find out, she sat down and went methodically through the stubs. When she had finished she was unaware that she gave a great sigh of relief as she tucked them back into the drawer. Had she really believed she would find the tell-tale evidence of regular payments made out to Walt Marlow?

So it seemed that there was no money involved. Kate stared unseeingly at the window. She was no nearer a solution. Yet there was something. ... But what? Besides, Walt's threats to herself had not left much to the imagination. He had blatantly threatened her father's happiness. So what did he stand to gain?

Kate knew a sudden longing for a friend, someone in whom she could confide, ask advice, someone who could tell her how best to lift the shadow that had settled across her father's and her own life.

With the thought the image of Brad Sheridan floated across her mental screen and she gave a start. Why should she think instinctively of him? He had caused her very first moments of unease concerning her father. And Marlow had warned her against him. Why? Where did Brad Sheridan fit in? And why had Marlow made that outrageous demand?

Kate turned away abruptly. If Walt Marlow only knew ... He had no need to enforce *that* stricture. Not after last night. Brad, and Elaine Winton ... Brad and his excuses ...

The return of Benny at that moment interrupted Kate's ceaseless worrying at the problem. Almost thankfully she went into the kitchen and checked through the programme for the day. She had just decided to give in to restlessness and go down into town when Fay arrived.

Kate made coffee and settled down to listen. Fay was usually bursting with news of some kind, and today she was almost trembling with excitement as she looked at Kate over the rim of her cup.

"Have you heard yet? About Elaine?"

Kate's breath caught in her throat. "What about Elaine?"

"I think she's leaving Rex. She booked into the hotel this morning, just as I was leaving – it's my day off, you know – and she had three suitcases. Nobody seems to have seen Rex all weekend."

Fay paused, apparently taking Kate's silence for amazement. "He wasn't at the club last night, and their place was in darkness when we passed it on the way home. By the way, what happened to you?"

Kate looked into the bright curious eyes and felt she wanted to scream. Her voice sounded shaky and unreal to herself as she said slowly: "Nothing. I had a headache. Walt drove me home."

Fay looked disappointed at the terse response. "I thought perhaps you'd heard something."

"No, I haven't." Kate picked up her cup jerkily. If only Fay would go. She couldn't bear this gossip, not today of all days. She couldn't feel any genuine concern for Rex Winton; if all the portents were true, he would be better off without his beautiful self-centred wife. Elaine loved herself too much ever to give happiness to any man. And Brad Sheridan was with her last night. The last man Kate would have imagined losing his head over another man's wife. But doesn't this merely confirm my original judgement of his character, Kate thought bitterly.

"Well, that wasn't what I came to talk to you about." Fay summoned up a wry, winsome expression which Kate was beginning to recognise. She wasn't surprised when Fay leaned forward confidingly and added, "I hope you're in a good mood this morning – I've a special favour to ask you, Kate."

"Oh." Kate managed a smile, though inwardly she sighed. "What have you been up to now, Fay?"

"Nothing!" Fay's baby-soft flaxen brows shot up with outraged innocence. "I never do. It's Mrs. van Hahn – she's had one of her bright ideas."

Kate nodded. She had met Mahore's managing director's wife only once, but knew that this lady was possessed of many bright ideas and the boundless energy to match them. Quite a few members of the Mahore community were quietly thankful that she didn't spend more than a third of her year there.

"It seems she's taken up a new charity," Fay went on, "and she's going to organise a fashion show to raise funds. Also, she reckons that it would be a tremendous boost for the feminine personnel and the wives, being somewhat cut off from the rarified aura of the exclusive couturiers' circles. Actually, I think it's a super idea."

Kate gave a non-committal nod. It was true; the town provided little scope for couturier fashion in the European sense, although Kate herself loved the little Eastern boutiques and the glorious range of silks and vivid Batik prints which could be obtained. "When is she going to hold it, and where?"

"She's booked the hotel dining-room provisionally for the twenty-first."

"Of this month? But that's less than three weeks away," Kate exclaimed. "There'll be a good deal of organising, you know. It isn't just a case of importing a few trunkloads of gowns and half a dozen girls."

"I know," Fay grinned. "That's where you come in."

"Oh no!" Kate put out her hands with a gesture of repudiation. "I'm on holiday."

Fay's mouth sobered. "You don't have to. You see, Mrs. van Hahn asked me to sound you out, so to speak, see how you reacted."

"Why couldn't she ask me herself?"

"Because she didn't want you to feel under an obligation to agree, because of your father being an employee," Fay explained hurriedly. "Actually, I think she's awfully sweet. She knows you're on holiday, and so if you'd rather not be involved, you've just to say so and that's the end of the matter."

"I see." Kate bit her lip, a little surprised at this tactful if slightly devious approach. "What does she want me to do? Model?"

"I think so." Fay relaxed. "But she wants your advice on the organisation in general. Oh, yes, say you will, Kate. It'll be tremendous fun. May I tell her, then she'll get in touch with you herself?"

Kate hesitated a moment, then abruptly her mood changed. Why not? It might help to take her mind off the worry which beset it. It might also occupy some of her spare time and provide an excuse for avoiding two men she wanted nothing more to do with. She took a quick breath. "Okay, I'd love to."

"Great! I'm so glad." Fay stood up and reached for her bag. "Thanks for the coffee – will you excuse me if I dash? I've got to see a man about lunch!"

Now that she had achieved her purpose for calling Fay did not dally with last-minute lingerings. She made a vivacious exit, pausing to fan herself with exaggerated gestures as she stepped out on to the veranda and met the humid wall of heat outside the cool, air-conditioned sitting room. Kate smiled after her, watching her petite figure cross the garden and duck into her small car. But when the silence came again and Kate was alone her brief mood of interest ebbed as quickly as it had come, to be replaced by an almost unbearable surge of tension. Kate stood there, her hands tightening on the edge of the sliding door. Almost she wished she had called Fay back, asked for a lift into town, where there were people, shops, activity. The day stretched ahead, empty, lonely ...

Suddenly Kate came to a decision. She had to escape from the house today. Without pausing to reflect on the impulse she told Benny she was going to the lagoon.

"Pack me some fruit and a bottle of mineral water while I change." She did not wait to hear Benny's murmured protest, "There'll be no one there now, Miss Kate. How you get there, with no car?"

"I'll take the boat," she told him when she returned to the kitchen a few minutes later and unknowingly answered his question.

Benny betrayed disapproval. "The Tuan won't – "

"He won't mind," she broke in. "If he phones tell him I've gone for a swim and I'll be back by six."

She picked up the basket, thrust her towelling wrap into it, and pushed her sunglasses on as she went out. It was only about five minutes' walk down the track to the inlet where the Merrivale boathouse held the family's old motor cruiser. Kate checked the fuel, and without wasting any time she jerked the motor into life. The sea was calm and there was very little breeze to stir the heat of a deep brassy sun. It was an ideal day for taking to the water, and Kate felt some of her tension ease as she nosed downstream and out into open water.

This was the first time she had taken the boat seaward alone, but she had done the short journey along the coast so often with her father she was not in the least nervous. He had a habit of talking aloud as each landmark or buoy hove into view, and now, as she skimmed across the sparkling blue she could almost hear his voice. His habit had always amused Mrs. Merrivale, but since Kate had learned to drive a car and found herself giving way to furious mutterings when in a traffic snarl-up she understood why a man would sometimes talk to his car – or his boat. Now she looked ahead for the particular grove of casuarinas and a tiny islet which warned her she was nearing a shoal. She eased out into deeper water, and a few minutes later she was rounding a fringe of reef to sight the three big boulders that marked the entrance into the lagoon.

She slowed down, her eyes intent and her hands steady, until the choppy stretch of current was safely negotiated and she was within the calm green oval. The club beach was deserted, she could see no cars in the clearing behind the hut, and there were no craft moored at the landing stage. The only sign of life, apart from the ceaseless activity of the bird population, was on the far shore. On the little beach in front of the white villa some children played, and nearby a group of boys were about to launch an outrigger.

Kate's half-formed plan to head straight across to the little beach abruptly shrivelled. She turned the boat and made for the landing stage.

The club hut would be locked and she did not have a key, but this did not worry her. At the moment she had little desire for company. Her mood had changed already and the surge of loneliness that had beset her when Fay departed had spent itself. She knew only a need to escape from the nightmare worry into which she had plunged the previous evening, and some dimly sensed instinct told her that only by purging her mind of its tumult of fear, worry and despair would she be able to face up to the problem and seek an answer unclouded by emotion.

She went into the water and alternately swam and floated while she tried to convince herself that at least her father's problem was not financial. But how was Walt using his hold over the older man? What did he hope to gain?

At last she came ashore and sat slowly drying herself and applying lotion before she partook of the picnic lunch Benny had packed. She stared across at the white villa and tried to think of the fashion show planned by Mrs. van Hahn. At any other time the idea would have set Kate's imagination working instantly and she would have been full of enthusiasm at the prospect of helping to organise it, but her tired brain refused to yield any flashes of inspiration, and an underlying sense of unhappiness was persisting like a doggedly ignored pain from which there was no respite.

She packed her things back into the basket and lay face down, suddenly aware of deadly lassitude. She closed her eyes and pillowed her brow on her forearms, and within minutes the heat of the sun and the effect of her long sleepless night had taken their toll.

Far across the lagoon the boys climbed into their outrigger and sent it skimming across the shimmering water. Their voices came faintly, then faded, and farther away, beyond the reef, a coastal vessel chugged stolidly up the Strait, a ragged trail of smoke from its stack thinning like an untidy grey veil over the sunlit blue. Somewhere in the undergrowth a short distance from where Kate lay there was a sudden violent commotion of monkey business. Their squeals and screams and chattering ran through the bush, a brilliantly-hued parakeet rose with an indignant squawk, and a flutter of tiny birds rose above the palms like a cloud of bright feathers. But Kate heard none of it. She slept unmoving, while the heavy swell of the Strait began to lap the bleached grey fringe of the reef, deepening the ridges of coral to wet pink and sending the lazy ripples of the lagoon into the strong, purposeful swirls of an incoming tide.

A long exploring wavelet almost touched Kate's bare, sand-veiled toes, and a darkness blocked out the sun from her reclining body. A voice said: "You'll get wet in a minute."

Kate stirred, sensed the coolness of shadow before the voice registered, and started into a half sitting up position. One hand went out defensively and she blinked up into the impassive features of Brad Sheridan.

"You! When did you — ?" Her heart gave a great betraying leap, and the exclamation of shock rushed to her lips before she could stop it. Then she remembered, and turned away, raising one hand to smooth her hair back from her brow as she said coldly: "I didn't hear you."

"I'm not surprised — you were a long way away. Just as well I arrived."

"Is it?" She fished her comb out of her little waterproof vanity case and disciplined the errant wisps, her smooth, unhurried movements giving no hint of the tremors not yet subsided within her.

He stood there, his stance unconsciously arrogant, and watched the long comb-strokes through the dark glossy tresses. "Did you come here alone?"

"I did."

She dropped the comb back in the bag and drew up her knees, wrapping her arms round them and staring at the shifting patterns of greens and blues and iridescent sun-gilt on the water. The silence lengthened and she was acutely aware of his gaze burning down on her studiedly indifferent profile.

"Tell me if I'm interrupting anything," he said at last, on a note of sarcasm.

"The beach is free." Her expression did not flicker.

There was another silence. He did not move, and Kate felt tension building like a wall between herself and the tall, implacable man who towered over her hunched, defiant person. Then:

"*Kate!*"

She gave no sign of reaction to the controlled violence of his address. "Yes?" she said between taut lips.

"All right! I know you're mad at me. And I know why."

"You know more than I, then."

A flurry of white sand fanned out under his shoe as he moved fiercely. "Listen, Kate, if it were anyone else . . . anyone else but you, I wouldn't explain."

"I'm not asking for explanations."

"But you're going to get them," he gritted. "And if ever you let one word slip . . ."

"I said I don't want to hear them."

"I'll personally flay that lovely rear of yours, and take the greatest pleasure in doing so."

"In other words, to twist a classic cliché, you'll add injury to insult."

74

Kate's mouth snapped shut on the words and she scrambled to her feet. Pointedly she turned her back on him and snatched up her belongings, intending to storm along the beach to the landing stage and make her escape. The next moment an iron grip fastened round her wrist and her wrap was torn out of her hands. Brad flung it down on the sand and said tersely: "Sit."

She stared up at him with furious eyes, and felt an impact that was almost physical as her glance locked with his. Anger glowed in his grey eyes, his mouth was set in a hard, inflexible line, and every line of his body seemed charged with power and determination.

"I've just stood up," she snapped.

"And you're going to sit down again, until you listen." His voice held the danger of quietness.

The pressure on her wrist was increasing. Slowly, mercilessly, he was exerting sheer brute male dominance, forcing her to sink to her knees or topple sideways. Utterly in control, he sank on to strong haunches and kept her hand pinned on the soft blue folds of the wrap.

"I'm well aware of what's eating you – and you got a mistaken impression last night. You think I deliberately stood you up yesterday." His face was within inches of her own, compelling her to listen.

She made no response, her expression cold and closed.

"And I've no doubt that the gossip-mongers had a field night at the club," he went on explosively. "Elaine Winton was ill."

"Was she?" Kate's voice was expressionless. She looked pointedly down at the hard tanned fingers that still bit into her wrist, and he followed her glance, then raised his glance to her, almost like a warning as he released his grip. Kate sat stiffly, rubbing her smarting wrist, and averted her head.

"Somebody had to look after her – she wasn't in a fit state to be left."

Kate drew a deep breath. "Listen, I've neither the desire for a flayed rear – as you so charmingly put it – nor to hear about Elaine Winton. I'm not sufficiently interested in your girl-friends."

"Elaine is not my girl-friend. She happens to be Rex Winton's wife, and I intend to see that she stays that way."

"Well, for what it's worth," Kate turned and met his angry eyes, desperately trying to maintain a cool indifference, "Elaine doesn't appear to have much intention of behaving like a good little yes-girl. She booked into the hotel this morning with three suitcases."

"My God! You women don't waste much time, do you?"

Kate ignored the disgusted implication. "So you see, the great secret isn't a secret any more. Now," she got smoothly to her feet, adjusting the straps of her bikini, "I'm going to swim. I suggest you get back – you might be needed."

She took only one step forward before Brad seized her arm and yanked her round to face him.

"That's unworthy of you, Kate. Elaine was drunk last night, and on the verge of hysteria. I had to see her safely home."

"Of course." Kate's expression betrayed nothing of the sick cold misery in the pit of her stomach. "I'm not disputing your action, Brad. I understand. Now let go of me."

"That's just it! You don't understand."

"Does that matter?" Kate prised his fingers free of her arm. "It doesn't to me."

"Elaine's pregnant."

"What!" The terse statement shattered Kate's precarious control. A stab of anguish constricted her throat, and for a dreadful moment she thought: Oh, no! Not – not Brad ...

"This is the basic cause of the trouble. She doesn't want a child. She's made Rex's life hell these past two weeks."

The clipped phrases sounded curiously far away. Kate was aware of a relief that was almost a pain. She couldn't have borne it if Brad, and Elaine ...

Brad's mouth compressed. "Rex reached the stage this weekend when he couldn't take any more. He lost his temper. They had a furious row that ended with Elaine having hysterics and storming out into the night. Rex had a forgivable reaction. He poured a drink and thought: To hell, let her cool off, then came to his senses when he realised she'd fled out in only a flimsy wrap over her nightdress. When he went out to look for her he couldn't find her, and no one had seen her nearby. He panicked, and rang me. I went over straight away, knocked up the Maddisons to see if she'd gone there. They joined in the search, and ten minutes later we found her huddled in that ornamental pagoda affair at the end of the Maddisons' garden."

Brad paused to draw breath. There was a white tautness at the corners of his mouth, and Kate felt tension in her own clenched hands. "This was – when?"

"Saturday night, very late. Early yesterday morning, actually," Brad went on. "Elaine was in a state of collapse. We carried her indoors and Lena put a fresh nightdress on her while we phoned the doctor. He gave her a sedative and got her settled down. We cleared out then, and left Rex sitting up with her. Apparently she was sleeping quite peacefully, and Rex lay down to rest at about four in the morning. But he fell into a deeper sleep than he'd intended, and the next thing he knew was the houseboy waking him to broad daylight.

"It was then he found the note from her, saying she was leaving him, she was going home for good this time." Brad paused. "I was on my way to collect you when I got two messages, one from Rex, the other to say there was a breakdown at the plant. As you know, that's Rex's pigeon as engineer, so I'd no option but to volunteer to take care of that while he went after Elaine."

Some of the hurt was leaving Kate's face now. She exclaimed, "But how? There's no flight from here to Singapore until Tuesday. How would she get there?"

"That was the problem," Brad said grimly. "We checked every timetable we could find, and could only conclude that she'd set off for K.L. And the thought of Elaine loose in a car over that distance nearly sent Rex berserk."

"She took the car?"

Brad nodded. "That was the worry of it – you know what a reckless driver she is. Then Rex remembered the Harmons – I don't think you know them – an Australian couple Elaine took up with a while back. He's involved with a government training scheme, minerals, at Bahru Pekan. Rex had a hunch she'd make for them. We couldn't get them on the phone, and I knew Rex

77

was aching for action, so I told him to take my car and see if she'd gone to them. By the time I'd sorted out the bother here it was lunch time, and then I felt bound to hang around within reach of the phone. It was almost sundown when he rang, to report a blank. The Harmons weren't at home, he'd rung K.L. airport and they had no booking for a Mrs. Winton. He was then setting off on his return journey. Would I hold the fort here, just in case there was any message? Naturally I agreed." Brad's shoulders moved with his deeply indrawn breath. "And that's why I had to let you down yesterday."

Kate made no response.

As though he was reading the trend of her thoughts, Brad leaned forward. "I don't know where the hell Elaine had got herself to all day yesterday. By the time I caught up with her she was in no fit state to tell me. I can only conclude that she'd had second thoughts, had returned home, to find Rex missing, me missing, the houseboy not to be found, and the Maddisons gone for a drive, and had hung around for a while and had another fit of temper. I got the shock of my life when I walked into the club last night and saw her there, high as a kite, announcing to everybody in general that Rex was leaving her and obviously determined to drink herself silly. I had to try to reason with her, and finally persuaded her to let me take her home. And that was where you came in."

His glance fixed on Kate's face, and she nodded. "You hadn't much option, had you? What about Rex?"

"He's back – so pathetically thankful that she's safe that I felt like spanking her. He desperately wants this baby, and wants to make a success of his marriage. I suggested that he should let her go home for a few weeks, until she comes to terms with the idea of motherhood. He didn't sound very enthusiastic about the idea, but I persuaded him it was his only hope. We're on the brink of the monsoon season, and frankly, I doubt if Elaine's temperament is strong enough to stand it. To put it plainly, she's unstable at the best of times; pregnancy, and this climate might cause a tragedy." He hesitated. "We've enough trouble at Mahore as it is."

The sincerity in his tone was undeniable. Kate looked away.

She felt vaguely ashamed of her readiness to suspect the worst of Brad, but her pride would never allow her to make such an admission. Slowly she turned her head and there was a slight raggedness in her voice as she smiled and said lightly: "Well, that's one little chapter you seem to have brought to a successful close."

"Not quite." There was a clipped quality in the objection. "I went back to the club last night, to find you, to explain and apologize. But you'd gone. You left with that – that flabby, objectionable ... Why didn't you wait?"

"For what? For the slim hope that you might – *might* come back in time to salvage the last hour of the day?" Kate flared. "Did you really imagine I'd sit around for the entire day? Just in case you changed your mind?"

"That's unreasonable!"

"It's not!"

"It is!" Brad's own temper flared in instant response. "Surely your own instinct, if not your sense, told you that something was wrong. I did send you a note, to save you the inconvenience of a wasted day. But when you walked past me last night ..." He released a pent-up breath and looked as though he was having great difficulty in refraining from shaking her. "Is that all you have say?"

"What do you expect me to say?"

"When I think of you with – with that – "

"Oh, so you do think occasionally," she taunted.

"*Kate!*"

There was a world of warning in his tone, but she chose to ignore it. Something drove her on, something she scarcely thought to question or restrain. "Yes, but you seem to have forgotten something," she cried. "You're the one making the issue out of this. You're the one who started it. I didn't create a fuss, demand explanations, expect you to – "

"No, but you got them. And you're getting this!" he gritted savagely, and seized her by the shoulders.

Kate had no chance against his determination or the violence of his kiss. Her slender body was crushed like a fragile stalk against his hard, unyielding strength as his mouth roved over her lips, and then, as the frantic evasive movement of her head left it defenceless, the soft column of her throat.

She gasped his name, a protest, and felt only the response of his chest heaving against her as he groaned, "Why must you always fight me, Kate?"

He bore her down on to the soft yielding sand and stared at her pale, distraught face. "I'm beginning to believe you *are* human, after all. I believe you were jealous, last night."

"Jealous? Of you? Because – " Kate's lips trembled with outrage. "You're crazy! You're – "

"Last night that calm of yours cracked when you looked at Elaine and me." Brad's hands pressed her down, forcing her into submission, to listen, and a wild exultancy glowed in his eyes. "It was the one thought that made me find you today. I had to find out. Because I couldn't stop last night – the explanations were too involved. There were too many people ... And I didn't know what Elaine's reactions would be. Oh, Kate," his hand tangled roughly in her hair, "stop tormenting me, and yourself."

For a long moment his darkened eyes searched her face, and suddenly, with all her heart, Kate wanted to give up the fight to keep Brad Sheridan out of her heart. The events of the past twenty-four hours had strained her nerves to snapping point, and now, in all the shifting sands of doubt and despair, he seemed like a rock of safety she longed to cling to. Her lips parted tremulously, trying to frame a response, and then he shook his head. "Don't say it, Kate."

The dark outline of his head blotted out the sky. She saw his shadowy eyes deepen with a searching intensity, as though they tried to seek out every thought and emotion in her own, and the clean firm line of his mouth became a sweet, infinitely desirable magnet as it hovered within an ace of her lips. Suddenly she was caught in a spell, and in one last weak attempt to resist its enchantment she turned her head to one side and pressed her face against his shoulder.

"Is that all I'm to be offered?"

But there was no cynicism in the quiet question, only a nuance that was halfway between tenderness and resignation;

certainly a nuance she had never yet heard in Brad Sheridan's voice. She returned in a whisper: "I'm not bidding, Brad."

She felt the sigh ripple through him, sensed his unwilling humour, and heard his voice against her hair: "Sweet Kate, you're no shrew – but do you ever give in?"

His hands tangled in her hair and tugged gently at the lobe of her ear. The sensuous touch was infinitely more dangerous than his former anger, and it took every shred of her resistance to quell the slowly rising tumult within herself. And then a swirling force surrounded her, and the skies above seemed to open.

Neither of them had noticed the storm clouds sweeping down the Strait, nor heard the hot sullen sighing through the trees. The crash of thunder and the impact of Brad's mouth burst on her senses at the same moment, and the rain-filled wind lashed across the lagoon.

Kate felt the sting of flying sand against her arms and the pitting of rain flurries on her legs. A resentment came fiercely, against the storm that screeched its warning to all humans to fly from its rage, and then, before primeval instinct to shelter could win, Brad moved, and the weight of his body came over her.

"Too late – it'll be over in ten minutes."

He sounded glad, almost triumphant, and then his mouth sought her cheek, her brow, her eyes and her temple, and uttered a sigh before repossessing her lips.

The wild fire of response consumed the last shreds of Kate's resistance, and the wild heart of the storm seemed to enter into her very bones, bringing a strange, crazy exultation. The rain was descending in torrents now, soaking Brad's thin shirt, making her skin wet, and moulding her hair to her head like a glossy black skin. The sand clung to her, rasping under his fierce hands, but she was conscious only of this new liquid fire of emotion. She met his kisses now, straining into his embrace and revelling in the hard muscular warmth of him under the plastered wet skin of cotton, giving herself up to the pulsating rapture of his lovemaking.

The storm raged above the two intermingled figures on the

pagan beach, as though the elements sought to vie with racing senses and the roar of the thunder to echo the throb of Kate's pounding heart. She did not know what he murmured, or what murmurs her own throat made in response, until the long possessive caresses sweeping down her slender body suddenly paused, and his breath stilled a moment. Kate quivered, felt his hand encounter the sand-caked ridge of her bikini top, and then seek to thrust away the frail barrier of nylon.

"*No!*" Kate jack-knifed back into sanity.

She huddled away from him, her breathing shallow and rapid, and her entire body quivering uncontrollably. With fingers that seemed scarcely to belong to her she adjusted the thin straps of her bikini top and pulled the wet clinging strands of hair back from her face.

Behind her Brad was silent. She willed him not to move or speak until she regained a measure of control, and gradually the world swam back into focus. The clouds hung low in the sky, turning the lagoon into a great oval mirror of sullen steel, and the wind whipped up racing flurries of white foam across the Strait beyond. Inland, the casuarinas moaned fitfully as their feathery crowns took the brunt of the elements, and the sound was like a tormented parody of the anguish in Kate's heart.

Then Brad spoke gruffly: "I suppose I should have expected that."

Kate drew a tremulous breath. "I'm sorry if you're disappointed."

"Oh no, disappointment is scarcely the word to express my feelings at this moment."

"And of course I don't have any!" she cried, stung.

"That possibility does occur to me."

"Then it's a pity it didn't occur to you a little sooner," she flashed.

She heard him move, and fear that he might touch her made her snatch for her wrap and scramble upright. The garment was scarcely wearable now, soaked and coated with the powder-fine sand, and as she tried to shake it reasonably free she found Brad standing in front of her. He put out his hands, and instantly she backed away. His hands dropped.

"Kate, don't let's quarrel."

"Quarrel?" Surprised, she stared at him, fully expecting to see cynical amusement replacing sarcasm. But he betrayed neither, only a somewhat enigmatic expression of query in his eyes.

"Yes. Because I came here to talk to you."

Kate swung the wrap round her shoulders. "You have a most eloquent turn of speech," she said unsteadily.

His mouth compressed, then apparently he decided to ignore the acid in her tone. He said quietly: "Shall we agree to say that I'm not the first man to be aroused to desire for a beautiful girl; and you are not the first woman to exert her privilege to change her mind at the last moment?"

For a moment she stared at him, almost uncomprehending, and he stepped forward, taking her silence for assent. Then he touched her arm. "Let's get out of this. I need a shower, even if you don't."

He looked so cool, as though he'd just bumped into her in the most conventional of circumstances, that Kate began to feel bewilderment. He was turning towards the clubhouse, a short distance along the beach, and she drew back. "It's locked. It's no use – "

"I've a key – and a change of clothes in the utility." He put a firm hand under her elbow, propelling her towards the shelter of the clubhouse veranda. "Wait here, I'll only be a moment."

Still a little dazed by his abrupt change of tone and behaviour, Kate stood on the veranda and watched him take long brisk strides round the angle of the building, to where she could see the bonnet nose of the vehicle parked in the clearing alongside. Suddenly she realised that the storm had almost passed. The clouds were thinning, the wind was not so boisterous, and the rain was subsiding to isolated flurries. She also realised that she felt slightly shivery, damp and untidy, and decidedly miserable. When Brad came back she made no objections when he opened the door, went to his locker and extracted two clean towels, one of which he pushed into her hands, and gave her a push towards the shower room.

She was not sorry to pee off her uncomfortably sand-encrusted bikini and shower her body free of sand and sea and rain. There was also a strange, more subtle element of cleansing, as though the ritual might also wash away the mixture of shame, regret and anger she was now experiencing. The strength of her own emotions was deeply disturbing. She had wanted Brad very badly during those moments of madness on the beach, and she felt almost ashamed of her weakness. It was all very well to assure herself that he had forced his attentions on her; but it was not entirely the whole truth. Some force within herself had overridden sanity and control, and he could hardly have failed to detect her weakening. What did he think of her now?

She could hear the shower sounds from the other cubicle, and their briskness seemed to express only practical male concentration on the job of the moment. Kate dried herself and towelled her hair as dry as possible, then suddenly realised her appalling lack of clothing. What on earth had possessed her to come out without additional garments? She had known she was going to swim, and that the weather was so unpredictable now as to exclude the practice of lying in the sun and drying out within minutes. But as the thoughts passed ruefully through her mind she heard a step outside, and then a robe was tossed over the top of the louvre door to the cubicle.

"Afraid this is all I can supply, but you can borrow it if you like."

"Thanks." With the muffled acknowledgement she took down the white and maroon towelling robe and donned it, fastening the girdle tightly round her slender waist. It was voluminous on her, but she was glad of it, and after quickly rinsing out her bikini she emerged, to find Brad in the lounge, busily mixing drinks at the bar counter.

He had also rescued her beach mules. Brushed free of sand, they lay on a stool, and she felt oddly touched as she thrust her feet into them. The robe was beautifully clean and dry, her damp hair was already drying into soft cloudy tendrils over the deep collar, and the sharp sting of the drink he handed her acted as an instant stimulant. She was beginning to feel normal again.

"Thanks," she murmured, "I needed that."

"You're not the only one," he responded dryly, and immediately she felt the warmth of colour flow into her cheeks. But he was not looking at her. His gaze was reflective on the amber swirl of liquid in his glass, and she dared to relax slightly. He hooked a toe under a chair, drew it nearer and subsided into it. He had changed into crisp, newly laundered bush pants and a cotton safari jacket that hung open, revealing his broad, teak-tanned chest to the waist. As though sensing her glance he looked up at her and smiled slightly. "I rarely travel far without a spare kit – not in this climate. The original boy scout – always prepared," he added mockingly.

"Prepared for anything, it seems," she dared.

"It's been known to pay dividends." Coolly he reached over and took her glass, topped it up, and handed it back before returning to his lazily relaxed position. "Kate, how long has your father had this close association with Walt Marlow?"

The question shocked with its suddenness. "I'd hardly call it an association," she said stiffly. "They've been working colleagues for years."

"Let's not quibble over words. Friendship, association," he shrugged, "call it what you like. But there has been a fairly close relationship between them for several years."

"So what? Why do you ask?"

"I have to. Has Walt Marlow any kind of influence, or hold, over your father?"

"What!" The golden rim of liquid swayed perilously near the edge of Kate's glass. She stared at him with eyes dark with shock. "What an appalling question to ask!"

"Is it?"

"Yes! And one that you've no right to ask."

"On the contrary, I have every right."

Kate felt ice form down her spine. With dreadful foreboding she remembered, and realised that Brad Sheridan had certain rights. That he was at Mahore for an express purpose – to investigate something as yet only secretly hinted at among the personnel. She gripped the stem of her glass with taut fingers. "Maybe you have," she said unevenly, "but you have no right to demand my answer. I have to remind you, for the second time, that I am not an employee of Mahore Latex. I can only suggest that you ask your questions at the pertinent source; either Walt Marlow himself, or my father."

She stood up jerkily and put her glass down with a sharp rap that sounded like a pistol shot in the silence. "And now I have to get back – it's late."

"Not yet, Kate." Before she reached the doorway he was there, barring her way, tall, broad, and suddenly implacable in his power.

"Listen to me," he snapped, "and stop looking at me as if I were your number one hate pin-up. I know exactly what's rotten in the state of Mahore. I know how! And I know who! But I need proof."

"Why come to me? A visitor?"

"Because I know your father's happiness means a great deal to you. And because nothing will convince me that you're totally unaware of something going on. Because wherever I go I meet a wall of silence, evasions, people clamming up the moment I ask a question that's getting near the bone," he said with savage intensity. "Everything is apparently running as smooth as syrup, while every pointer back at H.Q. indicates otherwise. Do you know that for the past five years Mahore has consistently shown a fifteen to twenty per cent drop in output in comparison to our five other holdings in Malaysia and the Indies?"

Brad paused, then put his hands on her shoulders. "Take it from me, I don't care who's involved, or how important they are, I'm going to pin the guilt on the culprit. If you've any suspicion, or know more than you'll admit of what I'm talking about, you've got to tell me."

She recoiled from the ruthlessness in his eyes, even as the dark coils of fear tightened round her heart. Suddenly things began to fit into place, bringing not only dread but a new kind of pain that was entirely personal.

"No." She shook her head desperately. "I don't know. I wish I did, for my father's sake. But if I did, you're the last person I'd confide in."

She struck at his hands, thrusting them away from her, and

anguish raged in her eyes. "This is why you followed me here today, isn't it? This is why you were so eager to make love to me! You wanted my confidence, and making love to a woman is an infallible method of bringing her to the point of total indiscretion. Well, you've wasted your time, and you've failed. And I'm glad!"

Kate slammed out of the club before he could stop her and sped along the beach to the landing stage. Uncaring that the cockpit was awash with storm-water, she scrambled in and set the engine to life. Tears clouded her eyes and agitation robbed her fingers of dexterity as she cast off the moorings, but somehow she got away without hindrance.

The storm had cleared now, as though it had never raged, and the westering sun shot a vivid blue sky with rose and gold pearl. But it brought no warmth to Kate's heart. Under the fresh fears that Brad's revelations had brought she could find only one small anguished consolation. Thank heaven she'd stopped short of making herself the biggest fool of all time.

*Will you never learn?* she asked herself savagely. *Paradise is built of illusions.*

# CHAPTER FIVE

KATE got home to find two messages awaiting her. One was from Mrs. van Hahn, with a return number and a request to ring back that evening. The other was from Walt, to say he might be a few minutes later than arranged but he would be there before eight.

She crumpled the note, wishing he would be a few days late – or preferably a few weeks; she was in no mood for Walt's company tonight, she thought furiously. She checked the time; it was not yet evening but she might as well try Mrs. van Hahn's number right away. She might be in.

Mrs. van Hahn was in, and she answered the phone herself, giving an exclamation of pleasure when Kate gave her name. The voice at the other end was charming and softly modulated, without any of the overbearing tones Kate was partly prepared for, and which might have been expected from a woman who held a certain amount of reflected power. But Mrs. van Hahn sounded sweet and unassuming, with an undertone of enthusiasm for her project which made Kate warm to her instantly.

"I suppose tonight's far too short notice – you're sure to have a date," Mrs. van Hahn said, and paused.

"I'm afraid I do have an engagement tonight," Kate confirmed, wishing with all her heart she could break that unwanted date. "But I'm free all day tomorrow, if that's any good."

"Tomorrow would be marvellous. Will you come in the morning, then have lunch with me?"

The arrangement was made, and when Kate put the phone down she felt some of the enthusiasm Mrs. van Hahn had communicated. It would be exciting to help organise a fashion show, and it would help fill some of the time that was beginning to hang rather heavily on her hands. Now, thinking about it, she was fervently grateful that she hadn't been idiot enough to turn down the request. Already ideas were beginning to bubble up in her imagination, and she went straight to her room, armed

88

with notepaper, to begin jotting some of them down.

The time flew, and the next thing she knew was her father's voice exclaiming, "So this is where you are!"

The absorbed expression faded from her face, to be replaced by the apprehension she could not help whenever she greeted her father after an absence. But although he still looked tired and strained, he managed his smile, and she hastily gathered together the sample programmes and estimates of costs which she had drawn up.

"You're going to take it on?" John Merrivale asked.

She nodded, and told him about her telephone conversation with Mrs. van Hahn, but omitted an account of how she had spent the rest of the day. As she showered and changed for the evening her spirits began to ebb, and again she wished her father would take her into his confidence. It seemed so ironical that each should be forced to withhold confidence, each with the motive of love behind the silence. If only they could face this secret nightmare together, face Walt's threats, defy him to continue his monstrous blackmail. If only she could tell her father that nothing, *nothing* would make any difference to her love and regard for him. But the bitterest obstacle of all could never be surmounted; their love for Mrs. Merrivale. No matter what, she must be spared heartbreak. And Walt knew this . . .

When he arrived, a few minutes before eight, smug and burly in a white tuxedo, Kate felt a loathing like a sick revulsion in her stomach. Did he really imagine she could ever contemplate even an amiable relationship with him, let alone friendship? Still less anything closer. But it was simply vanity as far as Walt was concerned, and the desire for power. If only he would keep his paws off her . . .

His solicitous attentions made her want to scream. He helped her on with her wrap, opened doors for her, adjusted the air-conditioning in the car, turned on the stereo cassette player, and every movement was an excuse to caress her bare arm, touch her, bring his face near to hers . . .

"I thought we'd go somewhere different," he announced as they neared the outskirts of the town. "I'm sick of the crowd at the club. Same old faces . . ."

For once Kate was in agreement with him. Brad Sheridan was almost certain to look in at the club sometime during the evening. The thought of encountering him, especially while in Walt's company, was daunting. "Where did you think of?" she asked.

"There's not much choice, I'll admit. I can't say I fancy the hotel – not while our chief Pooh-bah and his wife are in residence." There was a trace of a sneer in his voice. "That's the hell of this place; you can't get away from the job."

Kate looked out at the garish lights and activity of Mahore coming to life for the night. She did not care where Walt decided to eat; all she wanted was to get the evening over and done with, and pray that she would escape lightly from the petting session to pay at the end of it.

"What about Ah Chan's place?"

"That would be lovely," she said politely. "I haven't yet had a meal there."

"You shall now, hon," he reached across and patted her knee, "and one to remember."

He was in jovial mood as he escorted her into the amber dimness and tinkling chimes of the Green Pagoda, the newest night spot in Mahore. The food was varied and extremely good, and the wine list more comprehensive than Kate had expected. Walt ordered lavishly, despite Kate's protest, and for the first time it occurred to her to wonder how Walt kept up with his lavish style of living. He kept two houseboys and a cook, he owned his hideaway up at Mas Telok, his new car must have cost a bomb, and his liquor bill alone must be quite phenomenal. At the end of the meal she discovered that Walt had yet another weakness.

Above the restaurant there was a gaming room. Flushed with wine and a mood of jovial show-off, Walt would not hear any argument. "Come on, I'll teach you to play Fantan – the game with the cards, not the silly guessing how many coins under the bowl that they sit and play in the alleyways."

Kate groaned inwardly with dismay. "I don't think we should. Even if you can afford it I can't. Remember, I'm not earning while I'm on holiday."

"I'll stake you. Come on, hon, don't spoil the evening."

"I've no desire to spoil your evening, but I – " Kate's voice trailed away and she caught her breath in an abrupt little exclamation.

"What's the matter?" Some of Walt's joviality was losing out to impatience. Then he realised she was staring past him and he turned his head to seek the cause of her distraction.

Brad Sheridan was moving towards the table in the adjoining alcove. Fay was with him, smiling radiantly and already making her way towards Kate and Walt.

"Hullo, you two! Small world!"

"Isn't it?" Walt grinned, putting a possessive arm round Kate, who had risen from her seat.

"But you're not leaving?" Fay exclaimed.

"No – I'm just trying to persuade Kate to have a flutter."

"Not gambling!" Fay pursed her mouth roguishly. "Oh, naughty!"

During the trite interchange Kate had remained silent, conscious of the chill, implacable regard of her silent antagonist. Brad's lean features might have been carved out of teak with ice chips embedded in sapphire for eyes. He looked at her as though she were some stranger he had not the remotest intention of acknowledging, and suddenly Kate's body turned traitor. It remembered the magnetic chemistry of a man's hands, hands now no longer strangers to its secret, tender responses, and it ached with an anguish of longing, bitterness and disillusion. With an effort that was almost a physical pain she assumed a brittle, careless smile, and shook her head.

"No, we're not risking our all, Fay. Actually, we're just leaving. Goodnight." Before Walt could make any response she walked straight towards the exit, looking neither to right nor left. She reached the door, and suddenly Walt was there, surprised and slightly out of breath after his hurried pursuit of her. She swept out, unaware of heads turning and admiration in male eyes, and at last uncaring of what her escort's reactions might be.

"I say, hon," he exclaimed, "no need to overdo it!"

"Overdo what?" She waited for him to open the car door.

"You know what I mean." He grinned. "I bet Sheridan didn't expect the brush-off direct."

"I don't especially care what he expected." Suddenly weary she subsided into the car and stared with shadowed eyes into space. Even the denial hurt. Well, she might as well get used to the hurt; there was little else to expect, she thought numbly.

It was a long time since Kate had allowed herself the indulgence of tears, but she was very near that weakness now. Her throat constricted and her eyes stung, even as stubborn pride rose to try to deny emotional stress. And to think that this was the break to which she had looked forward with so much joy. Oh, to turn back the clock!

But that was the wish of cowardice, she told herself. There was no way out she could see, except to tread the high wire of each day as it came. The past shaped the future, all she could do was never to forget the future being shaped now, to think only of her parents' future happiness and try to ensure that in no way did her present actions jeopardise their future; for the rest, it was in the hands of the gods.

Resolutely she held on to the desperate little promptings of philosophy as the car slid through the night. Somehow it helped her through the submission to the embrace and the kisses Walt expected as his reward for the evening, and somehow it prompted the tactful choice of words to persuade him to come in for a nightcap. He could scarcely expect to resume lovemaking in her father's presence, and nothing would tempt her out of the house once she was safely indoors. She shivered as she walked into the familiar security of the bungalow; for how long would she succeed in keeping Walt at arm's length . . . ?

\* \* \*

The meeting with Mrs. van Hahn next morning was like a blessed return to normality.

She was a slender, still pretty woman in her mid-fifties, with a charming informal manner which was only slightly belied by the shrewd and lively intelligence in her blue eyes. The moment Kate arrived and was shown to the van Hahn's private suite in the hotel Mrs. van Hahn enquired if Kate would prefer coffee or an iced drink, and then ordered accordingly. When the tray of coffee was brought the two collaborators settled in the cool, air-conditioned sitting room and began their discussion.

Mrs. van Hahn was ruefully amazed at the amount of detail in Kate's preliminary notes. She reached out absently to the dish of crystallised kumquats and bit into one as she studied the list of requirements and Kate's rough estimates of costs.

"My dear, I never dreamed there was so much work and planning entailed. I sort of imagined that one simply asked an agency to send some models along, hired a suitable salon, and contacted a few exclusive dress wholesalers."

"Well, you could do a show that way," Kate restrained a smile – Mrs. van Hahn's words had so accurately echoed her own surmise to Fay. "But the facilities here are rather limited, and I imagine you want to try something more ambitious. Ideally, an original collection would make an occasion of it. But a lot depends on the cost available," Kate said delicately, "and also your contacts."

"I was hoping you might have some ideas about that."

Kate shook her head. "My contacts, such as they are, are mostly in London and Paris. As you'll know, the top couturiers have their own salons, and there wouldn't be any hope of getting a preview over here. I think the only answer is contact the buyer of one of the bigger stores in Singapore. You'd get a selection of the latest fashion-wear available out here."

"Singapore . . ." A thoughtful look drew a frown between Mrs. van Hahn's brows. She drew Kate's folder of notes back on to her knee and picked out one sheet. "I like this idea, you know. The two sections, one European, one Eastern, and then mingle them in an international parade for the finale. I also like your idea of an interlude with Balinese dancers and a gamelan orchestra. You see, I'm hoping to time this effort of mine to coincide with the Ecological Convention being held here next month. Of course it's partly political – almost every move one makes these days has to be. As you'll know, Mahore Latex is fully committed to doing everything possible to help develop Indonesian and Malaysian resources and economy – we're invested

93

up to the hilt in oil and minerals apart from our rubber holdings, and I hoped in my small way to encourage interest in the wives of the delegates who will be here for this convention." Mrs. van Hahn paused and smiled. "I'm well aware that a number of my friends back in Boston imagine that I trek into tiger-infested jungles and live in a longhouse whenever I join my husband here, and that's a notion I suspect quite a few of the delegates' wives may have too. Also, that was a pretty disastrous flood last month. I'd like to raise some funds for those unfortunates who lost their homes."

Kate nodded, and Mrs. van Hahn sighed. "But to get back to business . . . Would you be free to spend a few days with me in Singapore? There are several suggestions I want to follow up, and I'd like your expertise when I do."

Kate looked surprised. She had not expected this. "When?" she asked.

"As soon as possible. The Thursday flight if possible."

Thursday. That was the day after tomorrow. Kate hesitated, then thought: why not? Her father would not object, and Benny was perfectly capable of managing without her presence. And perhaps the trip would help her to get things into perspective again.

Possibly misreading the cause of her hesitation, Mrs. van Hahn added, "Naturally I'll take care of the expense side of the trip, my dear."

"I wasn't thinking of that, I – "

"But I'm forgetting! Your mother's having eye surgery and you're looking after things. I'm sorry – have you any news yet?"

"She should have had the operation by now – we're expecting to hear from my aunt any day now."

"Is she at Moorfield?"

Kate nodded, and Mrs. van Hahn leaned forward to scribble a note on a pad. When she straightened and turned back to Kate her smile was full of warm reassurance. "I'm sure everything is going to turn out fine."

"I hope so." Kate's mouth was a little tremulous. Although she had complete faith in her mother making a full recovery and regaining the sight in the affected eye Kate could not summon up the same faith in regard to her other problem and fear. But this dread was something she dared not share, not with anyone.

"Don't take on anything that's going to be burdensome — I realise now this is going to mean a lot more work and organisation than I imagined." The older woman's eyes held understanding as well as shrewdness. "I don't want to ask too much of you."

"No — I'd be happy to help," Kate said quickly. "I've always had a secret ambition to manage my own fashion show, just once."

"Well, here's your chance. And I'll be only too glad to have the benefit of your professional know-how."

"Such as that is." Kate gave a wry smile. "It's ages since I did a parade — I do mostly camera work now."

Mrs. van Hahn touched Kate's hand lightly. "Let's go and have lunch. And take your time to think over the Singapore trip. You can let me know later."

But Kate had already made up her mind. A couple of days of escape from personal pressures were exactly what she needed. Mrs. van Hahn was delighted and said she would make the arrangements straight away. Over lunch, the reason for the sudden thoughtful expression which Kate's previous mention of Singapore had evoked became clear. It was quite an involved little account, going back to the friend of a friend who had discovered the most wonderful Chinese dressmaker in Singapore.

"Well, we all know how clever they are, how one can have a suit tailored or a length of silk run up in next to no time for a very reasonable cost — although they don't do it for the song they used to." Mrs. van Hahn paused to refuse the addition of *sambal*, the fiery pepper sauce, to her *satay*. "Aren't you having *krupuks*, my dear? They're delicious!"

"I know," Kate was choosing chicken and rice, "unfortunately I come out in shrimp spots afterwards!"

"How horrific!" Mrs. van Hahn plainly had no fear of shrimp-spot after-effects as she helped herself to a generous portion of the little flaky chips of shrimp paste. "Well, to be frank, I was a bit sceptical about this marvellous discovery of Ellie's, then just before I left I ran into Rosalie Kelly – she's the wife of our eastern divisional manager – and she was wearing a really gorgeous affair. Made by guess who? Madam Kee Lun, of course!"

The name was unknown to Kate, and she waited until Mrs. van Hahn had taken a drink of her wine and drew a breath.

"Now Rosalie has a very difficult figure, so obviously Madam Lun must be a skilful cutter. And apparently she also designs. I have a hunch she could be the very person we're looking for."

Mrs. van Hahn certainly didn't waste time when she decided to back her hunches. She rang Kate first thing the following morning to say that all arrangements were made and a company car would pick up Kate at five the next day to catch the evening flight from Mahore Airport.

Kate told no one of her plans, with the exception of her father, who seemed delighted when she broke the news to him. He carried her cream travelling case out to the car, and enjoined her to have a good time and not to worry about him as the car pulled away.

As if she could help worrying about him, Kate sighed to herself, her excitement beginning to diminish as the old disquiet rose like the tip of an ever-present iceberg. And a new worry had occurred to her; what was going to happen when the time came for her to return to England? Already more than half her stay had elapsed. Her mother would be home, they would have a week or ten days together before Kate departed, but what then? It was unbearable to think of this monstrous situation remaining unresolved; her mother returning to find the same dark sense of foreboding still clouding their lives; her father growing more lined and strained with the threat of blackmail hovering above him; and Walt . . .

Then there was Brad Sheridan.

Would he still be present? With his questions and his investigation. His strange persistence . . . his unnerving inquiry into her father's association with Walt Marlow. How much did he know? How much information had he garnered in the course of his investigation? Dangerous information that had nothing to do with his main object yet could damage innocent people's lives if it were to fall into the wrong hands. Bitterness hardened Kate's eyes; Brad Sheridan was totally devoid of scruples. The day at Rainbow Lagoon had proved that. For a while she had been lulled, believing his sincerity and his concern for the happiness of Rex and Elaine, only to have her brief illusion destroyed. How many other women had he mastered, charmed, seduced, as a means of getting information which otherwise might never come his way. Pillow talk; the most dangerous talk of all ... Kate's lips whitened with the force of her resolve; Brad Sheridan would never succeed in his despicable attempts to obtain information from herself.

The car drew up at the hotel and Mrs. van Hahn emerged, immaculate in a beautifully tailored cream silk dress with ice-blue accessories. Her smile of greeting was warm and spontaneous, and Kate returned it, forcing herself to subdue her anxiety. It was always worse when she was alone.

The flight was uneventful and on time, and it was soon after eight-thirty when the landing indicators began to flash on in the cabin. Mrs. van Hahn stubbed out her cigarette, and Kate snapped into her seat belt, aware of her senses quickening. Singapore lay below like a giant carpet of glittering gems afloat in the deep purple night. Although Kate had visited Singapore many times the atmosphere of one of the major crossroads of the world never failed to excite her, and tonight was no different. The great city was ever-changing, there was always something new – even if only yet another towering block of concrete and steel had arisen where once had lain a motley alley teeming with colourful Eastern life.

Mrs. van Hahn had reserved a suite at Raffles, which delighted Kate, for she had not previously had the opportunity of actually staying at the famous old hotel which had captured the imagination and affection of generations of travellers.

After Kate and her hostess had showered and changed they dined in the Elizabethan Grill and discussed their programme for the following day.

"I think we'll put Madame Lun at the top of the list," Mrs. van Hahn decided, "because everything really depends on her.

If she proves a disappointment we'll have to start again from scratch."

But Madam Kee Lun did not prove a disappointment.

Next morning a cab took them through an intricate maze of little streets in one of the oldest parts of the city and eventually deposited them outside a tiny leather-worker's shop in an alley so narrow it scarcely permitted the passage of the cab. An urchin sprang up from nowhere and led them up a rickety stairway at the side of the shop. At the top he indicated a limply hanging bead curtain that screened an opening at the end of the dim-shadowed landing. Beyond, in an airless, box-like room, amid a rainbow clutter of dressmaker's patchwork, they found Madam Kee Lun.

The diminutive Chinese lady welcomed them gravely, and listened while Mrs. van Hahn explained that she wanted a special dress made very quickly. While they discussed materials Kate glanced round and bent to examine the partly sewed shirt which lay beside the sewing machine. The workmanship was faultless as far as she could see, but traces of her doubt still remained. So many Europeans came away from the big Eastern cities like Hong Kong and Singapore exclaiming with wonder at the glorious silks available and the amazing speed and skill with which a tailor would fashion a suit or dress. But the kind of collection Kate had in mind would need the flair and originality of a designer experienced in international couture. Were they to find that here?

An hour later Kate was excited as any tourist with her first silk bargain, and she had to admit her scepticism had been totally unfounded.

Madam Kee Lun invited them to take tea while the design of the dress was discussed and took them through to another room leading off from her workroom. The window shutters were thrown wide to let in such air as ever permeated the dense maze of overcrowded buildings, and beyond them was a tiny balcony with the inevitable line strung across to hold laundered garments. There was a couch on the balcony, and on it lay a young Chinese girl with beautiful delicate features that might have been chiselled from ivory, so pale was the petal skin.

"My daughter Kim, she is unable to rise to greet you," Madam Kee Lun introduced, with the stoic fatalism of the Asiatic. "She is crippled since accident five years ago. But she will draw dress for you, which I will make, and it will be right for you only."

Mrs. van Hahn was staring at the slender form of the girl, something like shock in her eyes, and Kate knew she had forgotten the main purpose of her visit. Then the shock went and concern replaced it, and Kate could tell that Mrs. van Hahn's thoughts were an exact mirror of her own. Did this poor child spend her life a prisoner of this hot, airless little room, an on-looker of the life that would by-pass her for ever?

"My dear, this is dreadful," Mrs. van Hahn exclaimed. "Can't they do anything at all?"

Madam Kee Lun folded her hands. "We try. Doctors try, for long time. But it is her back, you see. And once, lady like you, from America, tell us of western doctor who cure when all else has failed." For a moment something glowed in Madam Kee Lun's dark eyes, then it was gone and her expression became impassive again. "Where would we get money to go to western world? Kim, you see what honoured lady wishes."

But Kim was looking at Kate, and excitement had glowed in the delicate child-like face. While her mother was talking she had reached for a magazine from a heap of journals lying on the floor. Kate's own svelte form, swathed in rich mink, adorned the cover, and Kim was exclaiming unbelievingly: "*Kate?* You are here? Can I make gown for *you?*"

Her mother stepped forward and took the fashion journal from her daughter's eager hand. "No, you make gown for this lady. Do you think . . ." she lapsed into her own language, but the tone was unmistakeable, and a gleam of wry amusement came into Mrs. van Hahn's eyes.

She gestured to Madam Kee Lun and stood silently, watching Kim, who ignoring her mother's admonishments had picked up a sketching block and pen.

Already the sketch was leaping into life from the racing, talented hand of the little Chinese girl. Kate saw herself take shape on the blank white paper, her own long slender lines and graceful stance, the casual poise, the slight turn of the shoulders, the erect head, and as she watched Kim's pen added the long sinuously clinging lines of a floor-length gown. A few more strokes emphasised a high, choker neckline and two bands of braid marked the cleavage and the knee-to-ankle slit that added the perfect balance of the design.

Kate was astonished. She could see, as though it hung before her, how the completed gown would look, and as she looked down at the sketch Kim rummaged in a broken-edged cardboard box for more pencils. With a sure touch she etched in the colour, the delicate tints that distinguish Chinese art, then added the merest suggestion of a background, just the corner of a console table that made the drawing complete.

In style and presentation it was western, but Kim had blended in an atmosphere that was pure orient. She looked up at Kate, an eagerness in her eyes, yet there was anxiety there too, lest she had failed.

"It's beautiful," Kate said simply. "Who taught you to design like that?"

"No one." Kim's smile held shyness and a complete unawareness of her own talent. "I would get so tired, lying here, and one day I tried to copy a picture in an old magazine. After a while I found I could draw without copying, and I began to get pictures in here" – she touched her forehead – "and I start to draw them. One day a lady wanted a dress made and she could not decide how she wanted it styled. She look through all the magazines and not like any of the styles, so I try to make one that would suit her. Since then, I often draw a dress, and then my mother makes the pattern to the correct measurements."

"Have you any more designs?" Kate asked.

Kim had. From under the couch she produced a bulging folder and handed it over.

There were dozens of designs, a comprehensive portfolio of daywear, lingerie, casuals, sportswear, and some supremely beautiful evening and formal gowns. Some were purely eastern, some were frankly theatrical, and many showed the influence of the western design studied by Kim in the great magazines of the European and American publishing houses. But all were sketched in fine sepia outline and tinted with that enchanting delicacy peculiar to oriental art, and all had the unique touch of the little Chinese girl's great talent.

"Some of these never made, but on the back are details of best materials and kind of embroidery or special sewing needed," Kim explained in her lilting voice. "You see?"

Kate saw, and so did Mrs. van Hahn, who exclaimed her delight anew every moment. Madam Kee Lun prepared the tray of tea and little sweetmeats, but the scented liquid in the fragile cups cooled unnoticed as Mrs. van Hahn outlined her plans for her show and proposed that Kim should design the complete collection.

Madam Kee Lun seemed bewildered, almost unbelieving, but the business-woman in her soon came back to the fore. She had her contacts for obtaining the silks and materials, and she knew of seamstresses who could be engaged to help with the making up of the toiles and the actual garments.

"I still can't believe it," Mrs. van Hahn exclaimed when they were back at the hotel. "Tell me, Kate, am I being naïve in believing we've made a discovery?"

Kate shook her head. "I don't think so, in fact I – " she hesitated, her innate caution bidding her to wait until she had seen at least a couple of the designs made up before she committed herself to raising hopes that might possibly prove false.

"Say it, Kate. I'm discreet," the older woman smiled.

"I think Kim could have a great future," Kate said slowly. "I'd like someone to see this show. Buyers, fashion editors . . ."

"We'll get them." Mrs. van Hahn's eyes grew thoughtful. "Give me the names and I'll send the cables. At least we might get her some publicity. And then, if we could get Kim to the States . . ."

Kate nodded. She knew the unspoken thought. Perhaps this was the way to Kim's future happiness, the most priceless thing of all, the means of restoring her crippled limbs to mobility . . . Greater by far than the fame Kate's instinct told her lay in store for the little Chinese girl who spent her days on that lonely couch above a back street in Singapore.

*　　*　　*

They spent a week in Singapore, and by the end of it Kate was exhausted.

"I'm getting soft – too long away from work," she said ruefully that last night at the hotel, as they lingered over their after-dinner coffee.

"Odd!" Lorna van Hahn's brows quirked with humour. "I was blaming the climate. The only other excuse possible is the imminent onset of old age!"

"Mine, of course!" she added hastily when Kate smiled.

They fell silent, allowing the relaxation of tiredness to steal over them as they considered the ground and the preparations they had covered during the past hectic week. Kim had worked like a girl possessed, producing over a hundred rough sketches from which Kate had selected about forty to form the main nucleus of the collection. Madam Kee Lun had taken them to a silk merchant where most of the silks and brocades had been chosen from a positive wonderland of glorious fabrics, and the cottons had come from yet another merchant who showed a bewildering range of patterns. Three of the models had been engaged. They would travel to Mahore a couple of days prior to the show, and already several of the creations had reached the fitting stage. Kate, although she had not intended to model herself, had been unable to resist Kim's obvious longing to see her in several special designs and was going to take part in the final section of the parade. It would mean an added strain to that of producing and stage-managing the whole affair but she was aware of excitement and secret anticipation at the thought of the event. She also had qualms about the mounting cost. Even though this superb and original collection would cost only a fraction of a comparable collection by an established couture house, because of the fact of using an unknown designer and labour charges being so modest, there were still so many hidden costs to total. However, Lorna van Hahn seemed unconcerned;

she also seemed quite confident about selling the full quota of tickets at a quite outrageous price, and Kate did not doubt her determination to canvass her many friends in the area with a view to the selling of some of the collection.

Suddenly Kate was aware that her companion was speaking.

"Is there anything you wanted here, or anywhere you wanted to go?" Lorna van Hahn's voice was tinged with guilt. "I've just realised how I've monopolised every minute of your time while we've been here."

"No, you haven't!" Kate protested, a little surprised. "I've enjoyed it all, every minute."

"And I've left that afterthought until too late – forgive me for being so inconsiderate, my dear."

Kate shook her head. There was nothing to forgive. The crowded week had helped more than anything else to banish worry and fear. Now she was reminded of it all waiting for her back in Mahore. Nothing changed; nothing resolved ...

She looked up, to make the polite denial, and the words died on her lips. A man had walked into her line of vision. A tall man with thick dark hair above broad shoulders clad in an immaculate cream tuxedo, a man whose tanned profile was lean and strong, and achingly familiar.

Kate blinked, and an unsteady throb upset her heartbeat. It couldn't possibly be Brad Sheridan!

The man paused, glimpsing an acquaintance at a nearby table, and bent to speak to him. Kate saw him full face, and her heart plummeted into space. It wasn't Brad ... it was a total stranger.

With an inward groan of scorn for herself she wrenched her gaze away. How crazy could she get? Singapore mut be full of men who looked vaguely like Brad Sheridan from the back.

With regained calm she gave her attention to Mrs van Hahn. But the reawakened throb persisted along her nerve endings; she felt strangely divided. Half of her dreaded the return to Mahore the following morning. The other half could not wait to get back.

# CHAPTER SIX

A LETTER and a cable awaited Kate's return home.

The letter was from Aunt Rena, with the news for which Kate had longed. Her mother's operation had been completely successful; the bandages were off, and the eye surgeon was delighted with her progress. All being well at her subsequent check-up, Mrs. Merrivale would have another week with Aunt Rena before flying home at the end of the month.

"Thank heaven – oh, Daddy!" Kate flung herself into her father's arms and hugged him exuberantly. "Isn't it wonderful news?"

"Yes," John Merrivale agreed, but in so sober a voice Kate stared at him. Wasn't he looking forward to his wife's homecoming?

"I thought you'd be counting the minutes," she exclaimed.

He disengaged himself. "I don't want her to rush things or take any chances, that's all."

"Well, I should imagine the surgeon will tell her if it's okay for her to travel." Kate sighed, something in her father's expression causing all her joyous surprise to abate.

"And you know that it's the weekend of your fashion affair?" John Merrivale reminded her.

Kate hadn't realised it, and pleasure came back into her eyes. "She'll love it – if she does make it back in time. We'll have a celebration the next day, shall we?"

Her father nodded, but a little uncertainly. "I thought, Kate," he said at last, "that I'd meet her at Singapore and stay there overnight before coming home – she'll be weary after the long hop and it would give her more chance to get her breath back. Also, I was thinking along the same lines, of a celebration meal. What do you think?"

"I think it's a marvellous idea. Have a miniature second honeymoon, you two old love birds. As long as you get back for my special offering!"

Her father nodded again, but to Kate his demeanour did not carry the conviction of happiness that she expected. With a pang she noticed afresh how much her father had aged recently. His features looked drawn and thinner, and the lines at the sides of his mouth were deeply grooved by worry.

Kate bit her lip, a sudden determination insisting that she beg him to confide in her, but before she could speak he said abruptly: "You'd better read that cable – it needs an answer."

"When did it come?"

"Only this morning. Are you going, Kate?"

"I don't know." She was frowning, her oval face intent as she studied the somewhat lengthy communication

It was from Bart Benson, the head of a big agency where Kate was in great demand. It was forceful and explicit, and showed Bart's typical indifference to expense when he wanted something badly enough.

*"We have landed U.C. I expect your congratulations by return. We have three assignments for you. U.C. Silcona for A.B. slant. U.C. Thermatropic for technical. U.C. abstract for gen pop p. Locations Jamaica, Finland, London. Top rate. All exes. When are you coming back?"*

"It sounds big," her father commented.

"It is. Every agency in town would give its back teeth to capture Universal Chemicals' advertising contract – I must cable him back right away."

But what was she going to say to Bart?

Kate felt the old stirrings of restlessness and challenge return as she pondered the wording of her reply. Her mother would almost certainly be home by the end of the month, and the Mahore business for Mrs. van Hahn would be over. There was no logical reason for any vagueness regarding the date of her return to her career, except the purely personal one of leaving her parents again. And that had all been settled long ago. She had been blessed with understanding parents, who loved her enough to let her make her own life, and were wise enough to know that there was little scope for her in Mahore, except within the framework of the company, where Kate's ambitions had never lain. And after all, neither of her parents intended to end their lives out East, that old colonial trend was long since gone, and their retirement dreams were firmly fixed on a cottage in Kent, amid the cool green tranquillity of their homeland.

Kate sighed, and completed the form with the somewhat laconic message: "Involved here till 30th. Writing. Congratulations twice." Bart deserved them. This triumph would put him plumb in the middle of the big-time map.

She came out of the cable office, her brow furrowed. Why did she feel so uncertain? Why couldn't she commit herself? If she didn't seize this wonderful offer she must be mad! If it had turned up just before she left England she would have groaned with disappointment because she couldn't take it. So why didn't she walk back into the office and send off another cable, saying she would be home in a month's time?

Impatiently she tried to shake off the mood of indecision. She would contact Bart again within a few days. He hadn't given her an exact date, and he would be working on the assumption of her prearranged stay of three months. If there was any urgency he would have said so ... Meanwhile, she had more than enough to occupy her mind for the next couple of weeks.

She experienced a strange mixture of relief and disappointment when she heard that Brad Sheridan was away for several days, visiting another plantation farther up the coast. Kate resolutely immersed herself in the preparations for the fashion gala, knowing that despite all her careful planning there would inevitably be a last minute rush. Far better if Brad Sheridan remained at a safe distance.

A further two-day trip to Singapore became necessary, and Lorna van Hahn decided to make arrangements for Kim to be flown into Mahore a couple of days before the show. Madam Kee Lun seemed surprised at this idea, but Kate wasn't; she was coming to know the older woman more informally by now and realised the depth of her kindness and sincerity.

"How could we leave that poor child behind?" Lorna van Hahn said when they returned. "So what if it means coping with a wheelchair? I'll never get used to that fatalistic acceptance of the oriental," she added vehemently. "Just imagine, Kate, how you would feel if you were the inspiration behind all those glorious clothes and you couldn't see the full results of it?"

Kate could imagine this tragic possibility all too easily, and she hoped that at least one international item of publicity might result from the advance notices they had sent out. The local papers would report on it, of course, but if only they could get a mention in one of the top American or European journals it might open wider doors to Kim's future.

The warm friendship that had developed between Kate and Lorna van Hahn had not gone unnoticed, however.

"You're getting very thick with our esteemed chief's good lady," Walt remarked with a sneer one evening when Kate arrived home after dining with the chief and his wife. "She's only using you, you know."

"I don't think so." Kate kept her voice even. "It's entirely voluntary as far as I'm concerned."

"Oh, yes?" Walt's sensual mouth curled down at the corners, "just like the old army tradition? Who'll volunteer? You, you and you! It won't do you any good, Katy hon. She'll drop you like a hot cake afterwards."

"I won't be here very long afterwards, so it really doesn't matter." She looked at him where he sprawled in an armchair, making himself at home and free with her father's drinks tray, and the familiar surge of dislike tightened her lips. Why couldn't he get lost?

She kept her temper and made a small gesture with the portfolio of notes she was carrying, more for her father's benefit than from any feeling of politeness towards the unwanted guest. "Will you excuse me – I have to check through these before I turn in?"

Walt moved, reaching out and grabbing her hand as she was forced to pass his chair. He pulled her to a halt and smirked up at her taut face. "I will – on one condition, hon."

"And what might that be?" His hot fingers curling round her hand aroused a shiver of dislike. "Not another ransom – I'm penniless," she managed in a quiet tone.

"A preview of this parade of lush dollies who are about to descend on us."

"I doubt if there'll be much time for that, they'll only be here for a couple of days, three at the most."

John Merrivale laughed dryly. "You'll have to beat every male in Mahore in the rush, I'm afraid."

"And get past me." Kate pulled her hand free and made her escape.

At least she should be thankful for one thing, she reflected when she reached her room; the show was entailing a great deal of work for her, but it was providing a cast-iron excuse for avoiding any more socialising with Walt. For, in spite of his sneering attitude, he could not object too forcibly. Lorna van Hahn *was* the wife of Mahore's head, and her degree of wifely influence was an unknown quantity. Walt might grumble in private, but he was wise enough not to air impolitic views in public.

Fortunately in this same respect, fate seem to be working on Kate's side. The following day brought the company auditor, along with two more rather grim-looking senior executives who were strangers to the Mahore personnel, and this effectively kept the pertinent section of the staff, including Walt, fully occupied for several days. The post also brought the confirmation Kate and her father were awaiting; a letter from Mrs. Merrivale to say she was coming home as arranged.

Kate went down to the hotel in joyous mood. Today the carpenters were going to assemble the dais and catwalk and she wanted to make sure that these had been made absolutely firm and steady. There was nothing more nerve-racking for a model than to have to parade along a catwalk which either swayed or creaked, or worse, did both. She came out of the glare into the dimness of the reception hall, and almost crashed into the man coming out.

"Hello, Kate."

A gasp escaped her, and she recoiled from the strong hands that grasped her arms to steady her. Brad Sheridan wore a sardonic grin, and in a voice too low for anyone to overhear he said mockingly: "Still playing hate, Kate?"

"I haven't time to play anything – I'm too busy," she hissed. "Let me pass, please, Mr. Sheridan."

His brows went up at the icy accent she had put on the title, but before he could reply Lorna van Hahn came across the checker-tiled expanse from the wide old scrolled stairway.

"There you are, Kate – just in time." She smiled at Kate and glanced at the tall silent man. "We've got two strong new aides. Mr. Sheridan was afraid you might be having difficulties in explaining to the carpenters exactly how you wanted everything set up. Oh, and we've moved the work over to one of the company storage bays. Mr. Sheridan thought it would be easier."

"Oh," Kate said weakly, with a thin smile, "how kind of Mr. Sheridan."

"I understand you want to see to this today." His gaze dwelled on her with cool dispassion, and he indicated the car parked outside. "Shall we get over there right away?"

There was little Kate could do but acquiesce. After a brief exchange with Lorna van Hahn she turned and went out into the moist heat of the morning and the waiting presence by the car.

"I happen to be quite capable of telling the workmen how I want the job done," she said between clenched teeth. "And I also happen to know exactly what I want."

"Do you?" He put the vehicle into motion with unflurried movements. "I don't agree."

"And why not?" she flared.

"Because you know what you want but you won't admit it," he said with infuriating calm.

"We're talking about a business matter." Kate took out her dark glasses and stared at the mud-streaked track ahead as she donned them. "I fail to see anything concerning it which I should admit or not."

She sensed his slight shrug, and after a moment she asked: "I thought there were two of you."

"Rex Winton is going to see to the electrical side. We assume you'll need some kind of illumination."

Kate's mouth compressed. "I'd already arranged with the hotel management to have the use of some floodlights they have."

"Those!" Brad chuckled. "They haven't been used since the year dot. They were brought in for some special function when royalty once came here – probably Queen Victoria, judging by the look of them."

"I don't think she ever got this far," Kate responded tartly. "Mahore was scarcely on the map then."

"Judging by the look of the heap of scrap we inspected yesterday, that's the vintage, anyway." Brad drew into the parking bay and switched off the engine. "This way."

Grudgingly, Kate had to admit that there was more scope for the workmen in the big roomy shed than in the cramped little place at the back of the hotel where the set pieces were to have been assembled. Here there was the convenience of ample tools and additional labour if needed.

Brad walked over to the three men who waited and pulled a folded paper out of his pocket. Kate recognised it as her own rough sketch of how the dais and catwalk should look, and the miniature bamboo bridge she wanted for the background, which she had planned to bank with flowers and ferns.

He rested the paper on a bench and began to append notes and sketches of his own. Unable to restrain curiosity and annoyance, Kate moved to his side.

"I hope you aren't altering those."

He did not look up. "I'm merely translating your feminine version of construction details into something a carpenter and joiner can understand. For instance, how are you going to shift these without swiping everything within range? They may not need to be portable in a couture salon used specially for modelling, but in this case they'd be completely useless."

Kate bit her lip to check a furious retort. Some instinct warned her to postpone voicing resentment until he had finished. In all fairness she had to admit that she was hopeless at drawing, and she scarcely knew a hammer from a screwdriver when it came to anything to do with mechanical devices. She had always considered her best tool to be the telephone and then leave the rest to an expert.

Brad was rapidly sketching a plan of narrow battens crisscrossing each other that vaguely reminded Kate of the old children's game of cat's cradle. "These will form the base, and they'll open out or fold up in seconds, and the flat top will pin-hinge together and be perfectly firm and safe."

"As long as they don't wobble or creak," she said sharply.

"Anything I make doesn't wobble or creak – or collapse," he said coldly. "You have remembered that the dining room at the hotel, being the largest and most suitable place, will have to be cleared and set up ready for you in a short time. Twice," he added, almost accusingly. "You'll want a rehearsal the night before, I assume."

"Of course." Kate avoided his glance. "It has to be the dining room because of that big extension that opens right down the garden side. There isn't anywhere else that will hold up to a couple of hundred people. Any less number and the show will not make a profit."

Brad's mouth compressed. "I'm aware of that – and I've a rough suspicion of how much of this expense is going to be conveniently lost in company petty exes. Of course if you two ladies had chosen any other time but monsoon you could have held it at the club. The terrace and gardens would have been far more suitable. For your sake, I hope to goodness it stays dry for a couple of hours that night."

So did Kate, but she remained silent. Brad turned his back on her and began to issue instructions to the men. In a few minutes the shed was filled with noise of sawing as the work got under way.

She was forced to concede that when Brad Sheridan started a job he wasted no time. Nor did he content himself simply with supervising. Kate, uncertain whether she was supposed to stay or get lost, perched on the end of a packing crate and watched him pitch in. The heat was intense, and after a few moments he paused to strip off his shirt and fling it down before he resumed measuring and sawing off the lengths of batten. Sweat glistened on his tanned body, and made it gleam like polished teak, and suddenly Kate was aware of how she was watching the ripple of muscle playing across that magnificent back and powerful shoulders as he worked.

She caught at herself and dragged her gaze away, delving into her bag for a tissue to dab at the beads of perspiration that had formed on her brow. A shadow fell across her, and she looked up into Brad's enigmatic eyes. At once she was conscious of him, and a tremor shivered through her. But there was nothing enigmatic about him as he said curtly:

"Never mind the beauty repairs. What about some refreshments?"

Kate stared, and he said impatiently: "The canteen isn't far – you can see the office block over there – the canteen's next to it."

"Oh, you mean you want me to fetch you a drink or something?"

"That was the general idea." Arms akimbo, he loomed above her, and the familiar twin imps glinted in his eyes. "Carlsberg for me; tea for the boys here, and don't be all day about it."

Her oval face a study of her suppressed feelings, Kate went to do his bidding. Some ten minutes later she picked her way back over the rough track, failing to miss the sudden rain shower that descended and soaked her as well as the white paper cover she had put over the tray.

The three Malays, who preferred their tea to alcoholic refreshers, flashed their smiles and thanks to "Mem", but Brad gave her an unsmiling nod as he took the cold-misted can and flicked the ring off the top. He took a long swig, sighed with pleasure at the bitter chill, then said: "You can push off now, if you don't want to hang around. Be back about four."

"Me? Here?"

"You. Here. So long." He put down the can and turned back to his work bench as though she didn't exist

Kate hardly knew whether to laugh with ironic disbelief or cry with sheer rage. Men just didn't treat her like that! This new facet of Brad Sheridan's personality astonished her: she had experienced his arrogance, his magnetism, his charm and his forcefulness, but this was the first time she had met up with his own unique blend of indifference and insolence.

She was in an unusually subdued mood by the time she got back to the house. A shower and change of clothing did a little to restore her shattered self-esteem, but nothing towards soothing her ruffled feelings. Pride abhorred the thought of returning at his behest; common sense told her she had no choice. He had assumed a new authority, one she was unable to deny – unless she could make the damned things herself! – and there wasn't a thing she could do about it.

When the appointed time neared Kate set forth armoured in every protection her training had taught and that the climate would permit. Her dark lustrous hair swirled neatly round her face in a firm style proof against any downpour. Her flawless skin was devoid of make-up, but a transparent scarlet colour glossed her mouth, and her waterproof eye cosmetics had taken all of fifteen minutes to apply. She wore a white linen sheath with a deep square neckline, white linen sandals with inch cork soles, she carried a pink raffia bag and a big pink and white umbrella of paper and bamboo, and she looked superb.

Many eyes followed her graceful walk along the main, flower-lined drive to Mahore's office block and returned their attention reluctantly to their work as she passed on towards the somewhat rougher terrain beyond the parking lot. When she reached the shed she paused, hearing the hammering sounds within, then walked into the broad opening.

There was a moment of dimness as her eyes readjusted after the glare, and a moment filled with the illusion of coolness. Then Kate stopped.

Two of the Malay carpenters were sitting on a big half-moon dais in the centre of the ground. From the dais a long catwalk some two feet high stretched almost to where she was standing. On the end facing her, arms folded, sat Brad Sheridan.

For long moments his eyes raked her from head to toe. Then he drawled: "You must have known."

"What must I have known?"

"Isn't it obvious?" He stood up and took a couple of lazy paces forward. "I have to hand it to you, sweet Kate; you always dress the part."

"I should look extremely odd if I didn't," she returned aloofly.

"No, I wouldn't say that. You'd look extremely decorative in any state – perhaps more so."

"If that's intended as a compliment, my acknowledgements, but it's not the kind I welcome." Head high, she walked coolly past him to inspect his handiwork. "You've been extremely quick."

"It's still rough. Try it."

She was acutely aware of him at her side, and suddenly she was more on edge than ever she had been during the many times she had repeated these identical actions before hundreds of critical eyes. He placed an old beer crate beside the dais to serve as a step up, and before she could avoid it he had grasped her hand as she stepped up on to the dais.

"Now walk," he ordered.

Slowly and deliberately she did so, the full length of the narrow rostrum, then a turn, and back along the ribbon of new white wood to the dais. There, she looked down into questioning eyes.

"It's fine, except for one place. I felt it give a bit."

"Show me."

She went back, in small quick natural steps this time, and pressed her weight where the rostrum swayed a little. Brad ducked under the framework, and presently he emerged, dropping a stick of chalk into his pocket. "It needs another pin hinge. I'll fix it. What colour paint?"

"White – a matt one, please."

He nodded. "It'll be ready by Friday."

"Thank you."

Before she could divine his intention he reached up and caught hold of her round the waist. Too surprised to struggle, she was lifted down and for what seemed a heart-stopping eternity was steadied within the circle of his arms.

In a strained tone she murmured, "Thank you. I – I'm very grateful."

"You're not, you know."

Encumbered by a bag and the rustling oiled-paper umbrella, she had only one hand free to try to break the grip around her waist. "If that's how you feel I'm not going to argue with you, But I'd be grateful if you'd allow me to thank the men. I'm sure they will be much less suspicious of normal sincere courtesy."

Perhaps he became aware of a certain silent interest in the taut little exchange which had taken place or perhaps he had merely grown bored with baiting her. Whichever it was, he released her, giving no sign of his response except a slight compressing of his mouth, and walked away.

Kate thanked the two carpenters and made her escape. But for a long while afterwards she could still feel the pressure of his hands burn round her waist.

\*　　\*　　\*

Four mornings later Kate saw her father off on the early flight for Singapore, then prepared for the final countdown to the show. Madam Kee Lun and her daughter had arrived the previous morning, the models had drifted in from their varied destinations to a hectic round of fittings and alterations to the clothes, and Mrs. van Hahn was elated by a sudden rush of telephone calls from the press and other interested parties.

The collection had surpassed all Kate's cautious optimism. All the designs lived up to their promise on paper, and the four she would model herself were superb in their line, fit and workmanship. One in particular she loved. It was a formal gown, a skin-fitting, floor-length sheath of deep sapphire lining a semi-diaphanous silver tissue which gave a shimmering blend of silver and blue as she moved, and the utter severity of the cut was contrasted by a flowing cloak effect made of dark blue crystal pleated georgette that swung from her shoulders at the back. The kind of gown for Glyndebourne, or a glittering West End occasion. A total contrast to the little day suit of heavy cream Shantung with coffee brown facings and wide bronze belt.

The preliminary run through went better than she had expected, apart from the inevitable snags, some of them unglamorously mundane. One model complained bitterly that the loo didn't work properly; another girl had broken out in an alarming-looking rash. Later it came out that she had eaten a large number of lychees on her arrival, and the hastily summoned doctor diagnosed an allergy and administered an injection, assuring her that the worst of the rash should have disappeared by the following day.

But the effect of the beach-wear she modelled was sadly marred, and the covert sniggers of a young London model, who should have known better, did not help. Kate did a hasty re-shuffle of her programme to allow for another girl to take over the unfortunate Lucy's place if the rash had not gone as hoped, and restrained her impatience when grumbling began about the air-conditioning.

"Where's all the steamy tropical heat we've heard so much about?" asked the pert little newcomer from London. "Look – I'm covered in goose pimples!"

"Somebody tell her the facts of life," chuckled Tara, one of the models from the Singapore agency. "Turn off that cold air for five minutes, ducky, and you'll sweat like a horse through all the finery."

Gail stuck out her tongue, then forgot her goose pimples. "Who's that gorgeous hunk over there?" she asked, in a carrying whisper.

Lorna van Hahn looked over her shoulder, and Kate followed the glance, to feel her heart do a crazy lurch when she saw Brad leaning nonchalantly against one of the fluted columns by the entrance.

"That's our Mr. Sheridan," said Lorna, and smiled at Kate. "I suppose he is very attractive – in a rather rugged way. But I can't quite see why he has such a devastating effect on every girl he meets."

Gail chuckled. Her expression held the pity of youth for an older woman. "We're not so shy about expressing our feelings these days." She lowered her voice and glanced at Kate. "I'm beginning to warm up now!"

Kate's smile of acknowledgement was strained. Brad had started to stroll towards the group of girls. His eyes searched her with the same rakish insolence of the day earlier in the week. But now there was the addition of challenge.

"I suppose you're going to give me my marching orders?"

"Oh, no!" Gail looked at him, her dark eyes slumbrous and openly inviting under three-quarters of an inch of false eyelashes. "*Please* don't march away."

"You see. Someone is expressing welcome."

"Don't get ideas, Mr. Handsome," Lucy said sweetly. "After a couple of hours among her own sex our Gail gets a trifle thirsty for change."

"Don't we all?" said Fay Slessor, who had strolled in from the dressing room, where she had been pressed into service as general dogsbody. "There's an awful red mark coming round your head, Brad."

"Really?" Brad gave a cynical grin. "It isn't my halo, sweetie."

"Meanie – who told you that one?"

Kate decided that the admiring circle of femininity round Brad Sheridan was due for a break-up. She said in a sharp voice: "I want to run through the Eastern Magic parade, girls. Then we'll do the International Finale. Quickly, please."

Grumbling a little at her unusually peremptory command, they dispersed in the direction of the dressing room, and Kate drew aside the curtain which concealed the attractive little bamboo bridge which was being used for this part of the parade. Rex Winton came to help, and tied the tasselled cords that secured the curtain, then went across to the temporary switchboard he had assembled to control the special lighting effects.

The gamelan orchestra began at a signal from Kate, and the first of the girls walked out from behind the bank of fern and blossom. She was Balinese, and superbly graceful in a swathed eastern dress with a diaphanous scarf of rainbow tissue floating from her arms. She crossed the bamboo bridge, reached the dais, turned, displayed, and made her exit as her successor appeared in coral silk with gold embroidery.

Kate watched intently, although the Balinese girls' timing and movements were faultless. Brad remained at her side, and she wished he would not stand so close to her, his forearm brushing against her arm as he turned to ask:

"When do you appear?"

"Not until tomorrow evening, in the final section."

"Too good to need a rehearsal, darling?"

The tone was deliberately needling, and Kate's mouth set. "No, simply not good enough to do two jobs at once."

A prolonged pause at that moment gave her the excuse to move away and investigate the hold-up. She made a note of a slight adjustment needed to ensure the hitch did not occur the following evening and when she returned Brad had vanished. Then she saw him at the darkened end of the long room. He was bending over Kim's chair, handing her a drink of something in a tall glass, and even through the shadows Kate could see the vivacious smile of delight that lit the oval features of the little crippled girl.

Kate experienced a flash of poignancy stabbing at her heart, and as Brad straightened and pulled forward a chair to seat himself by Kim's side his face came into Kate's view. Even the shadows could not mask the softening of that hard lean profile nor the tenderness of his smile.

Abruptly Kate's expression shuttered, and she became aware of an atmosphere of waiting. She gave her full attention to the job in hand and resolutely turned her back on the man in the shadows.

Brad Sheridan would never wear that expression for her . . .

\*　　\*　　\*

The bungalow felt empty and unwelcoming when Kate got in shortly after ten. There had been a heavy downpour as she drove back, and the short dash from the car to the shelter of the veranda had soaked her to the skin.

A weight of depression hung heavily on her spirits as she stripped off and showered, then donned a light wrap and made herself a pot of coffee. She shouldn't be depressed, she told herself firmly. The run through had gone far better than she dared to hope, and Lorna had been delighted. Everything was organised for the next day, the fresh ferns and flowers to be brought at the last moment to try to ensure their life for the evening, the volunteers who would help Madam Kee Lun with a meticulous inspection of the collection before the show started lest there should be the tiniest mark or crease to be erased, and already a lot of the delegates had checked in at the hotel. The only thing that remained was for poor Lucy to lose her spots!

It *had* to be a success. And her mother would be home in time to be there. She would be able to see clearly, without strain and those dreadful headaches should be ended.

That alone was a cheering thought, and Kate got up, aware of physical weariness, to go and rinse out her cup before she went to bed.

She was switching out the hall lights as the phone jangled into the silent house.

Kate's heart skipped a beat. Her first thought was of her mother, that something had gone wrong and her father was ringing from Singapore. When she lifted the receiver and heard Walt Marlow's voice she gave a sigh of relief. But the relief was shortlived.

He scarcely gave her time to respond, once he heard her say, "Yes – Kate here," and as the sharp words tumbled into her ear she felt bewilderment, and the first cold tremors of fear.

"Just a minute!" she cried. "Where are you, Walt? And what briefcase?"

"I'm at Bahru Pekan. I –"

"Bahru – but what on earth are you doing there? It's –"

"Just listen, Kate," he snapped. "I've got to have that briefcase. It's urgent. You'll have to bring it to me here – I know it's late, but I've been trying to contact you all day, and when I did get through to the hotel I had to ring off. Why the devil didn't you come to the phone?"

"But I didn't know! I didn't even know you'd left town. And I've been at the hotel all evening. You knew that I–"

"Oh, never mind. Now, listen. I left the briefcase on the floor of your cloaks cupboard. It's . . ."

Briefcase? Cloaks cupboard? Kate passed a hand across her brow. What in the name of heaven was Walt playing at? She knew nothing about Walt's private possessions.

"I left it there the night before your father left for Singapore. It's there all right, unless anybody's touched it?"

There was a note of alarm in his voice, and she said hastily "If you say it's there it'll be there. No one here would touch it. But I don't understand. Why –?"

"You don't have to understand. Just bring it here – you'll do it in a couple of hours. I'll be at the Green Farruda – have you got that? The Green Farruda, it's in Merah Lane, off Kelung Road. Ask for Mr Lynn. I've got to have that briefcase before the morning. Understand?"

"Yes, but –"

"Kate, you'd better not fail me . . ."

There was a click, and the line went dead.

Kate's cheeks had gone waxen. She stared at the receiver, then put it down unsteadily. Had Walt gone mad? Had she heard all that in reality? To set off for Bahru Pekan. At least two hours drive away, through that belt of jungle, tonight Now! And then look for a strange hotel in a strange town. She did not know Bahru Pekan. It had sprung up during the past few years, a new port with an industrial development area opening up behind it. She'd never heard of the Green Farruda, or Kelung Road . . .

She moved away, a chill striking through her thin wrap. The loneliness of the house seemed to press round her, mocking her fear and indecision. And no one to turn to for help. *You'd better not fail me . . .*

The echoes rang in her mind, cold with menace, as she ran feverishly to the cloaks cupboard. The swift scutter of a lizard made her start with fright, and the stirring of a branch outside the window shutter seemed to whisper of the black night waiting beyond. She looked round the little room with the wash basin and the row of hangers, then at the door of the cupboard known since childhood as the glory-hole Almost fearfully she opened it, saw the jumble of old possessions, the papers and magazines waiting to be thrown out, her mother's sewing machine, packed away when her eyes became too troublesome to allow the strain of close work . . . It had to be a dream. There couldn't be a black briefcase down there . . . But there was.

With a trembling hand she pulled it out from behind the

machine, holding it away from her as she put out the light and went back to the sitting room. So it was true. She hadn't dreamed it, and all her nebulous fears were crystallized into a sudden knowledge.

Something had happened. The something in which her father was involved, which was the cause of the dreadful lines of strain that had turned him into a prematurely old man, which had made him vulnerable to Walt's threat of blackmail all these years. And it was all in this briefcase.

She tried the lock, and was not really surprised when it refused to open. It did not take a great deal of imagination to hazard a guess at the contents. Walt's passport. His private papers, and the other things which would provide the damning proof of whatever fraud he had perpetuated in the business of his employer: Mahore Latex. Kate did not know what it was, and she had no desire to learn. She only knew that suddenly everything had come to a head. And Brad Sheridan had been the instrument.

Kate ran to her room and began to dress in old black slacks and a black cotton pullover. Through her fear a new emotion was emerging, that of desperate hope. Walt was getting out – where, she neither knew nor cared. All that mattered was that he succeeded. That he went away, out of their lives for ever, leaving them alone. And if this meant a nightmare drive through the night, then she would make it. That she might be compounding a felony did occur to her, but what if she didn't? How could she risk endangering her mother's happiness? All she dare hope was that whatever Walt's involvement in the business might have been her father's silence would remain undiscovered. For her mother's sake . . .

The sight of her bed had never been so tempting as she closed the door upon it, and the black night outside so eerie and uninviting. She banished the weakness and quickly gathered together a map and a torch and a few other essentials, and then, with an afterthought, took her small store of money from her drawer. She might need it. She locked up carefully and went out to the car.

Five minutes later she was biting her lip with despair and

anger as the car obstinately refused to start. Damn the thing! It had been all right when she drove back less than an hour ago.

For a moment she was dangerously near the tears of frustration, then suddenly it occurred to her to check the fuel gauge. It was well down, but not that far down . . . she had better fill up anyway . . . She got out of the car and went to get the spare can of fuel and a tin of oil. By the circle of light from the torch she topped up all levels and put the gas into the tank. The reek of petrol flowed into the night, mingling strangely with the heavy scent of the hot moist tropical darkness. Kate wiped her hands, clanged down the bonnet, and turned to move the empty cans. The air was very still and all at once she had a sense of being watched.

Did a shadow move beyond the black shapes of the oleanders? Did she imagine a stirring among the glistening leaves? Kate's eyes strained across the garden, towards the faint ethereal outline of the white fence and slowly round the sweep of shrubs to the dim shape of the bungalow. An insect fluttered out of the night and brushed her hand, and she gave a small exclamation of shock. But it broke the spell, and abruptly she dropped the cans on the ledge by the store shed. She had to keep a grip on her nerves. If she started being fanciful she would never face the task that lay ahead of her. She had to think of one thing only at a time; she had to get that car started.

She walked round the front of it, picked up the torch she had left lying there, and turned to open the car door. Only there was an obstruction in the way.

A choked little cry of shock rose in her throat as the black shape of a man loomed there before her eyes. A shape as ominous and disturbing and unmoving as the voice that asked calmly,

"Going some place, Kate?"

# CHAPTER SEVEN

"*You!*"

Brad Sheridan detached himself from the outline of the car and stared down into her white face. "You sound as though you were having difficulties. Need any help?"

"What are you doing here?" She recoiled and glared back furiously. "Do you always go around trying to scare people out of their wits? I –"

"Sorry." His white teeth glinted in a smile that held no true regret. "But the racket you've been making for the past ten minutes was enough to rouse the neighbourhood. What's the trouble?"

"There is no trouble!" she hissed. "All I've done is put some juice in the car. Now shift yourself – please."

"Must be a very heavy date." He showed no inclination to oblige, remaining with one solid hand planted against the top of the door she needed to open. "And a very late one."

"I – I left something behind. At the hotel," she improvised. "I have to go back for it."

"Fair enough. I'll drive you down. Helping a lady in distress, and all that kind of thing."

"I'm not in distress, and I'd hate to keep you from your manly beauty sleep."

"Oh, it's no trouble." He opened the car door, and to Kate's horror slid into the driving seat. "I'll just check that your feminine attentions have done the necessary."

She saw that he had appropriated her keys, and was sliding them into the ignition. She watched him jab the starter, and with true feminine illogicality hoped that he would have no more success than she had had previously. But her hope turned to disappointment as the engine turned over at his touch, to purr into soft smooth life.

"Okay?" He looked round.

Kate's teeth clenched. Why couldn't the beastly thing

do that in the first place? She would have been well on her way by now, instead of . . .

"Thank you." With an effort she remained calm. "But I'd prefer to drive myself."

"Of course. I've never been a man to despise a woman driver – until she gave me cause." A couple of seconds and a couple of lithe movements of his long legs shifted him along, out of the driver's seat and into the passenger side. He slewed partly round, so that he was lounging sideways, eyeing her and plainly waiting for her to duck inside.

But Kate was gripped in dismay, as though caught by some malign, inimical hand. Her heart began to thud with panic as the full extent of her impasse came home. Then she saw him mutter and grope behind his back, to pull out the black briefcase – Walt's briefcase! – which she'd left lying on the passenger seat.

He glanced at it, his face unreadable in the subdued light from the little roof lamp, and then put it down on the floor, resting it between his feet. The hand Kate had stretched out slowly dropped back to her side and the panic flutters stirred to wildness in her heart. *What was she going to do?*

She had no option but to keep this unwanted appointment. But Brad Sheridan was the last – and the most dangerous – man with whom to keep it. Her brain churned in circles, desperately seeking a solution and failing, while the seconds seemed to drag into hours. She was trapped, completely and hopelessly. What *could* she do? Short of physically throwing him out of the car.

The thought induced a reaction dangerously near hysteria as mentally she measured the long, solid shape of him. And now there was an infuriating expression of puzzlement playing round his mouth and shadowing his eyes with mockery as he watched her, and waited.

It was almost as though he knew!

Did he know? A tremor of fear passed down her spine, and with the jerky movements of impotent anger she stooped and slid in behind the wheel. She flicked on the headlights, reversed in the turning space, and headed out on to the track. Her oval features had tensed and set as though carved from cream alabaster but inwardly she raged. So she had an unwelcome passenger who was going to stick like the proverbial leech. Very well, two could play at that game. Brad Sheridan wanted a ride; he was going to get one – one that put paid to any thoughts of rest he might have had for tonight. After this delay it was going to be well into the small hours of the morning before she reached her destination. And when she got there. . . .

Kate dared not let her imagination ride too far ahead, nor wonder as to the nature of the questions which would come before long. Somehow when she got to Bahru Pekan she would have to dodge him. Surely, in the darkness of a strange town, it should be easy for a girl to slip away silently into the night.

She came out on to the main road that led into Mahore, and experienced a flash of surprise to see the streets still aflare with gaudy light and the motley populace – or a section of it – still abroad in search of amusement. But it wasn't all that late, she told herself, trying to instill confidence into herself for the ordeal that waited her before the night was over.

In a strange way, part of her, the craven, feminine part, was glad that the journey into the night was not to be made alone. She had no illusions about the nature of the conditions she might have to contend with; this was no well-paved, well-signposted highway that lay ahead, but a rugged, ill-defined track through jungle and wilderness with all their attendant dangers. It certainly completed the paradox, she conceded wryly, that the man she feared most at this moment should also be the one whose strong indomitable presence brought this odd sense of reassurance.

He was quiet now, but what would be his reaction when she flashed past the hotel and left the lights of the town far behind? She slowed outside the fairy hoop of lights that arched the entrance to the Botanical Gardens, waiting for the two cars in dispute there to end their argument, and Brad's sunburnt hand shot in front of her, to sound a critical blast on the horn. Traffic from the other direction was also held up, and there was the usual cacophony of noise before things began to flow again.

"Do you usually blow other people's trumpets for them?"

she asked coolly. "I'm not entirely helpless, you know."

"I know." She sensed his ironical grin through the note in his voice. "A third hand's useful occasionally, my dear Kate."

*Where you are concerned that could be true!* she longed to riposte, but quelled the impulse. An idea had occurred; if she could get him talking so that the moment of realisation might be postponed . . .

"Yours has been very useful this week, I must admit," she said in a softer voice. "I must also congratulate you on the marvellous job you've made of our background pieces. Several of the girls remarked how attractive that little bridge is." She saw the illuminated entrance to the hotel gardens looming ahead and went on hurriedly: "I always thought you were essentially a man of the great rubber outdoors – when you weren't tearing round the plantations sorting out the Company's troubles."

"There's more to life than rubber and Mahore, and maybe more to me than those – but then you've never troubled to find out, have you, Kate?"

"Life's so full of things waiting to be discovered, and time is very short." The car was abreast of the hotel now, and Kate put her foot down hard on the throttle.

The road shot away beneath, and the car leapt into the wide residential road that was the end of the town's built-up area. She found she was holding her breath, waiting for the fierce exclamation, the command, even the sudden masculine bid for control of the car.

But none of these came. Brad did not move, and though Kate did not dare take her eyes off the road she sensed he was looking at her. She also sensed that he was fully aware of what she had done. Then why didn't he say something?

"Life can also be very sweet – if you encourage it." His voice was even. "Kate, you're driving too fast."

"Scared?"

"Not particularly – you'll soon know when I am."

"I didn't ask you to come along, you know."

"My memory is as good as yours. *Kate!* – let's get there in one piece."

She saw that the needle was rising well over the eighty mark, and almost reluctantly eased the pressure of her right foot. The tremors of panic were beginning to flutter again, and suddenly she wished that he would start to argue, vent his anger even, anything but this calm icy acceptance which somehow was far more disturbing than any display of masculine temperament would have proved. Once again the frightening thought returned, that he knew. Knew where she was bound, and why.

But how could he know? She hadn't known herself until an hour ago. Unless ... could he have guessed? Did he know Walt had fled? Was he simply following a hunch, taking a chance that she might lead him to Walt?

A sick feeling coiled in a knot in Kate's stomach. She had been so preoccupied lately, with the show, and with the excitement of her mother's homecoming, she had scarcely spared any attention for the gossip and speculation which were part of Mahore's European community's daily life. She just hadn't listened to what was going on, or what rumour said might be going on ...

Suddenly she wished he would say something, anything, to break the taut silence that had bound her since his last chill directive. She stole a rapid glance at him, and saw that he was leaning back, his profile too shadowed to be readable, his gaze apparently intent on the road ahead.

Except that it was no longer a road. They were skirting the plantation now, and the sea had come into view on her left. Kate was forced to give her entire attention to driving in case she missed seeing a pothole before it was too late and the car suffered accordingly. Once she felt the back wheels start to slide, and was forced to drop her speed even further. She had passed the turning that led to the lagoon, and now the track began to climb more steeply through the jungle-clad hills. Soon she would reach the dip down to the bridge over Taikiang Delta, and as she mentally ticked off the landmarks for which her eyes were straining she remembered the last time she had traversed this route; the night Walt had brought her here and made his dreadful accusations.

She still hated to admit in her innermost heart that they could possibly be true, but the memory instantly served to harden her determination. Brad Sheridan or no Brad Sheridan, somehow she would get that briefcase to Walt, and pray to God that he would never again hold his vile threat of blackmail over her father's head.

During the next half hour Kate almost succeeded in forgetting her now taciturn passenger, until the suspicion began to grow that she had taken the wrong turning. It was all his fault; but for his unwanted advent she would have studied the map and made sure she knew exactly how to plan her route to Bahru Pekan. Instead she had driven straight off and had not dared to stop to study the map. Now she did not know where she was; she had long since left behind the more familiar terrain that encircled Mahore. She pressed on, however, telling herself that as long as she kept to the coastal track she must reach Bahru Pekan eventually. It was a port; therefore the north-bound track was bound to lead there.

She took a quick glance at her watch and was aghast to discover it was long after midnight. How much farther? And had she enough fuel? The gauge seemed hardly to have dropped, yet she felt as though she had driven for miles and miles racketing over bumpy track, straining and peering into the darkness, while her clothes assumed the familiar uncomfortable, stuck-to-her feeling.

"You know you've missed the Mas Telok turning?"

She started violently at Brad's voice.

"About three miles back," he added.

Kate recovered. "I'm not going to Mas Telok."

"Sure?"

"Why should I?"

"That heavy date I surmised." His voice was cold.

"You surmised wrong, then," she gritted.

The track was becoming narrower than ever, and her nerves were at snapping point with the strain of making sure she did not lose the track and land in a swamp. The terrain had been gradually descending for the last mile or so, and every so often she felt the viscid sucking squelch under the wheels. If only the moon would emerge from behind that blanket of heavy cloud!

She was beginning to feel as though she was trapped in the endless dark tunnel that the probing headlights were boring through the black tangle of forest.

It was wet as well. Trails of moisture kept streaming down the windscreen, and every so often the long clinging fingers of liana plucked at the side of the car, as though to catch it in a choking green net. And then suddenly she felt the car drop, and in the misted glare ahead she saw the great fallen tree-trunk that straddled the track some twenty yards in front.

She slammed on the brakes, there was a bloodcurdling crack from somewhere under the car, and at the same moment Brad yelled: "Look out!"

His warning was too late. Kate felt the car slither sideways, turning as it did so in a nightmare of slow motion, and then abruptly his weight was thrust over her as he reached for her door handle.

He was shouting, "Quickly – out!" and scrabbling to push open the driver's side door before Kate realised what was happening. Then the hot moist night air rushed into the car and he pushed her upwards with the sheer force of his own body.

"We're in a swamp! The track's collapsed. Get *out*, Kate!"

Fear brought impetus back to her shocked limbs and she struggled to obey, holding back the door that wanted to swing shut in her face as she scrambled out of the listing vehicle. She grimaced with distaste as her feet sank into mud and she almost fell headlong, clutching at the top of the door to save herself. Then she turned back.

"My bag! And the case!" she exclaimed frantically. "And the torch!"

Brad was already out. He plunged back inside and scooped out her handbag and the briefcase, thrusting them at her, and she saw that he held the torch in his free hand. He seized her arm and thrust her forward, stabbing the torch ray back in the direction they had come.

The track, or what was left of it, was a morass. Great twisted roots snaked across it, and there were huge potholes rimmed with earth that had caved in and filled with water. Somehow Kate stumbled out of the great mud crater and with Brad's help regained the comparative safety of higher ground. She stopped breathlessly, and Brad swung the torch-light back towards the car. It lay, slewed across the crater, already up to its axles in mud and mangrove roots.

She stared at it, her cheeks deathly white and dismay rapidly replacing shock. "What are we going to do? We – we can't leave it there. We'll have to get help."

"Where?"

She looked at his grim mouth and her own trembled. "But it's sinking. It'll sink further if we don't do something."

"And what do you suggest? Telephoning for the A.A.?"

She recoiled at the icy sarcasm in his voice. "I only asked! But at least I'm finding out some of those things you were so ready to accuse me of failing to discover."

"Be warned, then; you're liable to find out a few more before the night's over."

Bitterly Kate turned away and tried to shake the water out of her shoes. Several things were becoming painfully evident, the least of them being discomfort and a burning resentment of her companion as she realised the appalling truth. They were stranded!

A kind of desperation took possession of her. Suddenly everything felt unreal. She couldn't really be stuck here in the middle of the jungle, miles from heaven knew where, and with very little prospect of rescue. For even in the event of a vehicle coming this way during the night it was unlikely to be going in a direction of use to herself, even if the track wasn't now totally impassable with the cave-in and the tree. Kate sighed miserably. Instinct told her that Brad Sheridan was right as usual; the turning five miles back was indeed the main track and the one she should have taken. This one was probably a byway that wandered to a remote kampong; without a map it was impossible to tell if it ever meandered on and eventually rejoined the other track.

If only she hadn't been so startled by the sight of the fallen tree she might have noticed the ominous fissures in the stretch of track immediately ahead of her that spelled their own warning. And by the look of things a bit more was due to collapse. She could see the watery runnels seeping along as she bent to replace her waterlogged shoe, and she could feel the soft muddy earth giving beneath her feet. As though he had followed her thoughts Brad grabbed her arm impatiently.

"Never mind that – come on! Let's get out of here before we finish up to our necks in it."

With unceremonious haste he started to propel her along into the night. Because she could think of no better alternative Kate went without protest. If they could get back to the fork she might be able to get a lift to Bahru Pekan.

How she would elude her unwanted companion she did not dare to think, and within minutes she had ceased to worry about that problem. Before she had covered a couple of hundred yards the prospect of covering another nine thousand began to take on the magnitude of a journey to the moon. Every second step either skidded or sank into slime. The night insects gathered in clouds of joyous welcome about Kate's head, collecting a fresh batch of relations at every overhanging branch, a tiger mosquito homed on her chin, and her clothing stuck to her like a clammy second skin. The feeling of unreality had proved fleetingly transient and reality was hammering home its full horror. She would be lucky to get out of this by morning. She would never be able to deliver the briefcase in time, the results of which failure didn't bear thinking of, and she had wrecked the car. *How on earth was she going to break the news to her father?*

A second sting needled her face and the instinctive movement she made took her off guard for a second. She did not see the coiling root Brad had spotted in the light of the torch, and the next moment she had caught her foot and almost toppled headlong. Only Brad's instant grab saved her, and she clung to his arm while she regained her balance.

"Okay?"

"Yes, I think so." Then she gasped as she put her weight on her right foot.

He stood by, while she flexed her ankle and tested it cautiously, then he exclaimed impatiently: "For pete's sake – don't say you've bust your ankle?"

"N – I don't know . . ." She bit her lip and forced herself to take a limping step forward. "It'll be all right in a minute . . ."

"You'd better hang on to me. Here, I'll take those." He reached for her bag and the briefcase, and instinctively she clung to them, shaking her head in protest.

For a moment he stared down into her stubborn face, then his mouth set in a grim line. "Just typical stubborn Kate, aren't you? You never change. Come on. I only hope you find he's worth it."

Her mouth parted and shock widened her eyes. "What did you say?"

"You heard. But I'm afraid you're too late."

"I – I don't know what you mean."

"You do, but I'm not going to put it into single syllables now," he said brutally. "Now move, Kate."

Mechanically she stumbled forward while her frightened, tired brain tried to work out exactly what he meant. Again she felt the dreadful suspicion that he knew the purpose behind her wild journey into the night, that he guessed from the start. That was why he had persisted in accompanying her. Hadn't his voice been full of meaning when he told her she had missed the turning to Mas Telok? He had assumed she was going there to join Walt. But if that surmise was right he didn't know that Walt was much farther away than his former hideaway. Hideaway . . . Kate sheered away from the unfortunate choice of noun; it was too near hideout . . .

The dull throbbing ache in her ankle was only a fraction of the misery fast undermining even Kate's determined courage. The trek was becoming a nightmare; the black alien shapes of the jungle, the vines that snaked down to catch at her hair as she struggled on, trying desperately to match Brad's tough fortitude, plagued by insects, unnerved by the eerie drip of moisture everywhere, the sense of unseen life lurking, all whirling into the vortex of despair that spiralled ceaselessly in her mind. The briefcase, Walt, her father, the car, the briefcase . . .

And then the rain began.

The fierce, blinding tropical rain that slammed down like

silver sheets, shot with thunder and stabbed with lightning. It soaked Kate within seconds, and washed away the last shreds of her resistance. The cool, self-possessed civilised Kate of the hot-house world of the camera studio disintegrated like the delicate shell of a piece of shattered porcelain. Tears came into her eyes, to blend unseen with the rivulets coursing down her cheeks, tears caused as much by rage at her own weakness as by this last slam of a malicious fate. Only her pale lips stayed doggedly clamped together against betrayal of the secret, inwardly vulnerable girl she had always guarded from the world, and might have kept on guarding but for the advent of the man who had set out from the start to break down her resistance. Almost blinded by rain she did not know she had given an audible sigh of sheer weariness, until she realised that Brad had stopped.

She stared incredulously as he slipped his arms out of his jacket.

"Come on." He held it cape-wise above his head and gestured. "It'll keep the worst off for a little while."

She almost laughed outright. He was inviting her to come under the shelter of his jacket. The way her father used to huddle her close under the shelter of his arm and his jacket all those years ago when she was tiny and they were caught out in a downpour.

"What's the use?" She moved on, away from temptation. "I'm so soaked now that nothing could make any difference."

A whiteness flared round his nostrils. "No, because you're determined it shall not."

"I'm not going to waste breath and time arguing."

"I reckon you're going to have plenty of both tonight," he said dryly. "Notice anything?"

"Such as?"

He ignored the curtness of her response. "We're climbing."

Kate was too weary and dispirited to have noticed this until he pointed out the fact. Now she recalled the last five minutes of that nightmare drive, how the track had dropped downhill before she hit disaster. She gave a ghost of a shrug and resisted the temptation to dig at the burning lump on her chin. At least they were heading in the right direction of escape from this no-man's-land of mud and nature gone riot.

"It means, I hope, that we're not far from shelter." His hand urged between her shoulder blades. "I noticed what looked like a temple spire somewhere around here as we came down."

She bent her head against the onslaught. "I didn't."

"You wouldn't. You were driving. Come on, Kate, it isn't far."

She swallowed hard. If he said, "Come on, Kate", once more tonight . . . And then she felt his arm go around her waist.

It was warm and protective, and it was like a strong, iron-sure support that sent an irresistible temptation crying throughout her body. Her own arm went round him before her tired reflexes could deny the motion and she was drawn against hard strong contours that seemed instantly to lend their strength and endurance.

It was too late to withdraw now, and as they toiled up the pitted mud slope Kate conceded defeat and leaned thankfully against his solid frame. Stabs of pain were searing through her foot, and she knew that her strength was ebbing. Suddenly Brad stopped and looked into the darkness.

"I think this is it."

He played the torch to left and right, and Kate saw the rough clearing through the undergrowth. He left her, to go forward slowly, then he beckoned to her to follow. A little way ahead she made out the darker shape of a temple's curved roof against the night sky.

There was a gateway to the inner courtyard, and the sensed presence of ancient stone deities waiting in the dark, and then a broad flight of shallow steps leading up to the entrance into the main shrine itself, like a high dark slit in a veil of mystery. Kate shivered, and Brad gripped her arm.

"Be careful. These steps are crumbling and overgrown."

Kate tried not to think of snakes and spiders and ants and bats, all the unknown that might lie within that harbouring slit, as she picked her way up the rain-slippery steps to the terrace above. Then she saw that the terrace opened into a kind of annexe before the door into the temple. Brad paused, shining the torch around the floor and the rays came to rest on a low stone plinth down one side.

"Here, you'd better rest that foot for a while."

He folded his jacket and put it behind her back, then stood watching while she took off her shoe and rolled up the leg of her slacks. The ankle looked swollen but not unduly so, and she said uncertainly, "I don't think it's sprained."

"You probably ricked it badly. Stay there."

Before she could ask his intention he had turned and gone down the steps again, the torch light bobbing and fading out of sight within seconds. The darkness closed round Kate and she knew an instant need to summon him back, or hurry after him. Despising herself, she fought the craven desire, acknowledging that her trust in him in this respect was never in doubt. He would never desert her under these circumstances. Her fear was the ancient inbred distrust of the unknown at night.

It seemed an eon, although actually it was only minutes before he returned, holding a folded drenched handkerchief in his hand. He knelt down, probed her ankle with searching fingers, then bound the cool wet handkerchief into a firm binding around her ankle and instep.

"Leave your shoe off for a while, and I suggest you sit on this. At least it's dry – which my jacket isn't – and it'll insulate the chill of that stone."

Beyond the torchlight she could only guess at the irony in his expression as he held out the briefcase that was to make an improvised cushion. "Better?" he asked.

"Yes, thank you." She looked away from the light. "But we can't stay here very long."

"I think we have to." He seated himself on the plinth and stared out at the rectangle of night sky. "At least until first light."

"But we can't!" Her head turned sharply. "I have to – "

"Yes?" he prompted, as she bit back the unguarded betrayal.

"There are things I have to do."

"Like delivering that briefcase to Walt Marlow?"

Her indrawn breath was a gasp, and he said calmly: "Why pretend any longer? Marlow won't be coming back. And we know why he won't be coming back."

"I'm not pretending. And you've no proof that this briefcase belongs to him."

"Kate," there was ice in his tone now, "I have a very good idea of the nature of the contents of that case you're sitting on at the moment. If I were you I wouldn't protest too vehemently. I may decide to prove my claim."

"You'll do no such thing!" She sat bolt upright, her hands going down to close protectively over the edges of the case. "This belongs to me."

"At the moment, yes. But do you honestly think you could stop me?"

"Don't dare try!"

"I don't need to." Sardonic amusement touched his mouth. "It no longer matters."

A chill of dismay made her tremble. "What do you mean?"

"It's too late to matter."

His words made only an enigma, and served to deepen her misgivings. "Then why ... why did you follow me? Why did you insist on coming in the car, instead of making all that fuss?"

"For reasons which are entirely personal."

Kate licked dry lips. Did he suspect her of involvement in Walt Marlow's mysterious transgression? "I – I don't understand," she whispered.

"No? Then let's say you've left it a bit late to start trying."

He stood up and walked slowly out to the head of the steps. His tall figure stayed there, silhouetted against a clear night sky, then paced slowly out of sight.

The short-lived tropical squall had passed now, as though it had never been, but Kate scarcely registered that fact. She felt lost and helpless and scared, a prisoner of circumstances which seemed to have taken an unknown turn and over which she had lost control. Feverishly she drew the case out from under her and tried to force open the catch with trembling fingers. But the little chrome lock stayed stubbornly fast. She exclaimed under her breath, then remembered her nail file and groped through her handbag until she found it. A few moments later the tip of the little file was bent, and the briefcase lock had still refused to yield to the fresh onslaught.

"If you're really so curious about your own property, I could probably do that for you."

He had returned on silent steps, to loom above her, a dark inflexible force she was losing the strength to fight. She shook her head. "As you say, it's too late to matter. I – I think we should move on now. It's stopped raining, and the moon's getting up."

"I'm afraid you're unlucky, Kate." He dropped down at her side. "Unless you feel prepared to stumble along without this and maybe do in your other ankle."

He held up the torch, flicked it on, and she saw the radiance dim instantly to a thin red glimmer along the bulb's element. When she stayed silent he put the torch on the ground and said in an indifferent tone: "The only suggestion I can make is that you stay here while I go in search of the nearest habitation. I may be able to raise something in the way of transport. Then I'll come back for you."

"In a bullock cart?" She shook her head, unwilling to admit that neither alternative appealed in the least. All she longed for now was a car to step into, a bath, and her bed. And to wake up to a dawn from which all her problems had vanished.

But the dawn could herald only worse problems even than those which had worried her all these weeks. Her father would return, to the shock of this fresh development, of Walt Marlow's flight, of Brad Sheridan's final tracking down of the knowledge she had tried to conceal, and her own last disastrous attempt to avert the showdown. Her mother would be there, joyous at reunion and homecoming, only to find that the nebulous fears she had left had proved only too real. And there was the show . . .

"Kate . . ."

She started at the sound of his voice.

"It may not be as bad as you think."

The ominous words fell softly into the night. In text they sounded innocuous, almost soothing, but to Kate they seemed to underline her fears regarding the man who had given them utterance. How much did he know? How much that was still unknown to herself? The missing pieces that would fall into place to complete the picture she dreaded. She closed her eyes and willed him not to speak. If only her father had taken her into his confidence. Told her what it was he had been forced to keep silent about, and not left her to learn from Walt the reason for his silence. At least she would not have this awful sense of impotence, of treading on shifting sands, constantly afraid of giving away something that might further jeopardise her parents' future happiness.

"What time do you expect your parents home tomorrow?"

"On the morning flight," she said dully.

"With luck we'll get back before they arrive."

She caught the inflexion that suggested they might never know of her absence and shook her head bitterly. "I'm supposed to be meeting them. What about the car?"

"We'll use mine. And I'm hoping we'll be able to have yours towed out, although I suspect you cracked an axle on that bump just before we skidded into the swamp. We'll tell better in daylight."

She made no reply, save to huddle back against the stone and avert her face. She had no doubts about Brad's sincerity in this respect. He would be as good as his word; he would rescue the car, and he would provide transport to meet her parents. And he would get her home safely. But somehow this made everything seem worse. It didn't match up to the other side of his nature, the ruthless way he had gone about the job he had been sent to do, the way he had set out right from the start to probe into her life, to find out the things he wanted to know. And the way he had not scrupled to use the oldest, most despicable gambit of all: the undeniable man-woman attraction present between them from the first moment of meeting. But the strength had been on his side; the weakness on hers.

Brad had fallen silent. Kate stared at the patch of silvery landscape visible through the wide entrance. The late moon was well up in the heavens by now, and the edge of the entrance threw a strong black shadow, making a sharp line between shadow and silver moonlight gliding across towards the place where Kate sat. Presently Brad moved, and without warning leaned across and touched the binding round her ankle.

She started slightly, and he said: "It's almost dry."

"Yes."

"I'll soak it again."

"No – don't bother," she said in a muffled voice.

"It's no bother."

"No!"

"Why not?" His hand moved and touched the bare part of her foot, lingering in a way that was almost a caress.

She flinched violently away. "Don't touch me!"

"Why not?" he repeated.

"Because I don't want to be touched."

He shifted his position, resting his weight on one hand and looking down at her set face. "That's a pity. You're so essentially a touchable person, Kate. Don't pretend you don't know it." His voice deepened musingly. "Warm, smooth, feminine. The man who'd deny it is either a liar or a very feeble specimen of manhood."

"Maybe. I'm sorry I can't return the compliment."

"Too mean? Or too scared?"

"Neither."

"I think your fighting spirit is recovering, Kate."

"And I suppose you're going to take full credit for that," she said bitterly.

He sighed. "I wish you'd try trusting me for a change, Kate."

"Give me one good reason why I should."

"I will; the truth. Could it be that you don't trust yourself?"

She turned a scathing glance on him. "I trust my head, not my heart. But put on whatever interpretation you please," she said wearily. "It's still a free world."

"Is it? Then why does every meeting with you become a confrontation? To be riddled with analysis and shot up with inquests?" he demanded fiercely.

"Because the first may prevent the second." She stared into his shadowed features with disillusioned eyes. "And it's time you recognised a few home truths yourself, Brad. The confrontations, as you call them, have never been of my seeking, or making."

"They need never have been at all." Suddenly he leaned over her, his arm crossing her waist to make her a captive within its hoop. "Oh, Kate, do you ever relax and take a man on trust?"

Her body stirred instantly to his nearness. All the bells of her defence system started their clamour, while the traitor heart of her womanhood yearned for the touch of his hands. The conflict of sense and sensation forced her into the release of action. She thrust him away violently and jerked upright.

"No! Because I need to trust before I relax. And before I trust I need to respect. But maybe that doesn't mean anything to you." She stared into the night and the cold radiance of the moon sculpted her profile into frozen silver relief. After a moment of silence and his failure to respond, she added: "Does that answer your question?"

"In so many words, yes," he said at last, and his voice had gone very quiet. "But it isn't the answer I'm looking for, Kate."

She curled her hands tightly together. "I'm aware of that. I know you've one thought in your mind at this moment, as far as I'm concerned; you want to make love to me. That's true, isn't it?" Her voice rose unsteadily and she swung round to him with a scarcely controlled movement. "If nothing else, it would help to pass the night away, wouldn't it? Well tell me something! Would it really satisfy you to make love to me like that? Love without the added response of total commitment? A transient relationship, without trust, and without respect?"

There was an unnerving silence. Brad froze as though transfixed, and she could feel the aura of barely contained anger that surged from him. Somewhere in the distance a jungle creature screamed, and the sounds of the night began to steal back to people the void of that tense silence. Kate felt an iciness creep through her veins, making the numbness before the ache that was to come. Then she heard the hiss of Brad's indrawn breath and knew he had fought and won a battle of self-control. There were the slight scraping sounds of his movements as he got to his feet, and for a moment he looked down at her with darkened eyes. Then he gave a heavy sigh and turned away.

"All right, Kate. You win."

# CHAPTER EIGHT

KATE thought that night would never end.

When the echoes of his footsteps died away her first reaction was that of panic. She was alone. He'd gone. To make his way back to civilization, his male endurance and self-reliance perfectly capable of tackling the arduous trek, whether it was light or dark. She pulled on her shoe and limped out to the top of the steps, and there down in the darkness to her left she saw the wax and wane of a tiny red glimmer.

She stood there, her breathing quickening with relief, and waited until the pinpoint glowed again. Then the constriction of regret caught at her almost like a pain. She knew that Brad rarely smoked, and somehow that small, smouldering betrayal of weakness seemed to express a poignant loneliness.

Kate tried to harden her heart as she went slowly back to her resting place and the masculine cover of a still damp green bush jacket that was her only comfort. By the feeble glimmer left in the torch she checked her watch, saw that it was just after three, and settled herself down to wait out the remaining hours until dawn.

She must have dozed eventually, then fallen into an uneasy sleep, for suddenly a voice came reaching down into the dark realm of her slumber, calling her name, and a grasp on her shoulder jerked her into full wakefulness.

"It's time to move. Six o'clock." He straightened and waited while she equated herself to her surroundings and stretched her cramped limbs. When she stood up stiffly, to make an intent business of brushing at the creases in his jacket and handing it back to him, he said in a flat voice: "There's water down there if you want to wash. But don't drink it."

"I won't." She refrained from adding that she needed no warnings about drinking untreated water and moved in the direction he indicated.

She descended the steps and crossed the courtyard, veering

to the left where an uneven path led under the shadow of the great temple. She came to a low wall, perhaps the one where Brad had kept his lonely vigil, and stopped, unprepared by his prosaic words for the view that lay ahead.

There was a great verdant bowl with tiers of stone dropping down to the pool in the hollow, and a high rock face at the far end, pitted with old stone arches in which carved deities stood. The stone tiers were heavily encrusted with grey-green lichen and mosses, and silvered with the ribbons of moisture where water poured from hidden ducts and flowed into the pool beneath.

It was just light, with that curious cool stillness of the tropical dawn which was so shortlived. Mists lay in curling wreaths over the limpid surface of the water, and great clusters of lotus blossom lay like a pale rose carpet at one end of the pool. Beyond it were the temple gardens, a wild and pagan florescence of vine and leaf, streaked with the pink of hibiscus and the lavender fronds of tamarisk.

It was incredibly beautiful.

The rose and pearl reflection of the dawn sky came to lie on the mirror of the pool as Kate approached its edge, and it was instantly a cool and beckoning temptation. She longed to strip off her clammy, night-creased clothes and plunge into that inviting expanse. But it would take time, and she dared not risk the possibility of a certain onlooker . . .

She contented herself with splashing her face and arms, and sponging off as much as possible of the dried mud on her slacks before she combed her hair, applied the shield of a flaunting of bright lipstick to boost her jaded self-confidence, then returned to where he was waiting.

He had found some small tangy pineapples and sliced them with his pocket knife. He offered her some, with the brusque: "At least they'll quench the worst of your thirst. Sorry there's nothing more filling."

"I'm not hungry, thanks."

"I am." He peeled and sliced another for himself, and presently when Kate had had sufficient of the sweet juicy fruit, they set off along the track.

Kate was forced to admit that Brad was the most resourceful of men to be stranded with, and that had she been alone she would have had a great deal more difficulty and taken much longer in completing the return to Mahore.

After an hour's walking he struck off on another byway Kate would scarcely have noticed which brought them to a small kampong on the edge of a lagoon. While a crowd of naked, inquisitive children gathered round Kate, and the smell of cooking fish floated from the fire along the little crescent of beach, Brad arranged the first stage of the journey back. The whole village gathered on the beach to watch the strangers take to the water by outrigger, which Brad told her would save time. There was a trading settlement a short distance up the coast, and here he would be able to hire more conventional transport.

It was an ancient and dilapidated station wagon, and after the necessary discussion of terms it set off with Brad at the wheel, Kate beside him, and the vehicle's owner as passenger in the rear. It seemed he had intended to go into market anyway, judging by the assortment of produce, the crate of live chickens, and the two piglets which added their protests to the sundry creaks and groans of the ramshackle vehicle.

Every part of Kate's body ached by the time the outskirts of Mahore came into view. The familiar landmarks went by, and Kate felt as though years instead of hours had elapsed since she drove out into last night's darkness.

It was close on eleven when Brad pulled into the side lane leading to the Merrivale bungalow. Without waiting for the handbrake to go on Kate scrambled out and rushed across to the gate. Benny must have been watching. He appeared at the rear door and rushed out to meet her, crying frantic relief at the sight of her, and then shock at her appearance struck him temporarily dumb.

Kate had forgotten how she must look in her old, travel-stained black garb, and she said quickly: "I'm fine, Benny, don't worry. I'm sorry to scare – "

"Your foot, Mem Katy!" He had spotted the improvised binding round her ankle, a corner of which had slipped and worked its way down over her shoe. "What happened to you? Where have – ?"

"It's okay now – I'll explain later. Has there been any message? From anyone?"

"No, no messages. What do you want for lunch, Mem Katy? Not much time before – "

Kate reached the door, well aware of the lack of the time. She had scarcely forty minutes to get to the airport, and she had to clean herself up, and she had to try to contact Walt, before . . .

Her mind racing, trying to put priorities in their right order, she yanked open the fridge door. There was half of yesterday's bird . . . "Cold chicken and salad, Benny, and open a tin of fruit for afters." It wasn't exactly her idea of a suitably celebratory welcome home meal, but in the circumstances it was the best she could do. They would eat at the hotel tonight, after the show . . .

Still clutching the briefcase and her bag, she left Benny to get on with the lunch and hurried through into the hall. She grabbed the directory and rifled feverishly through the pages, her heart thudding as she searched for an entry for the Green Farruda. It would probably be too late, but she had to try.

She did not see the shadow cross the pathway outside and mount the veranda steps as she asked for the number, nor did she hear the brief exchange of voices out in the kitchen. She tapped her foot impatiently, waiting, until at last the line crackled and she heard the metallic tones at the other end.

No, Mr. Lynn had left. Very early this morning. No, they did not have any forwarding address. No, Mr. Lynn had not left any message . . .

The line went blank, and Kate felt weakness pervade her limbs. She leaned against the hall table and slowly replaced the receiver. Now what?

"I told you that you were too late."

She spun round as the quiet tones broke the silence. Brad Sheridan stood in the doorway, and suddenly she knew he had heard every word.

His cold glance raked her white face, then he came forward. "Can you be ready in fifteen minutes? The flight's due in on the half hour."

"Yes," she said tonelessly. "I'll be ready."

"Good. I'll snatch a sandwich while I change. Be with you in a quarter." He half turned away, then checked, almost casually, "Oh, I'm afraid I'll have to take this, Kate."

Before she could motivate tired limbs and stop him he picked up the briefcase. He reached the door, and Kate broke free from the trance of dismay. "No!" she cried.

He halted, his expression unmoved.

"Don't you care about anything – or anyone?" she flung at him.

"I care about many things," he said evenly. "Do you want a list of them?"

"No – I want that briefcase back!"

"So that you can destroy it?"

"If necessary, yes!"

He shook his head slowly. "I'm afraid I can't allow you to do that, Kate."

"Even if I tell you that it may contain something damaging to my father?"

"I'm afraid we'll have to take a chance on that." His mouth was grim as he watched her involuntary gesture of despair. "If I don't take it the police will."

"The police!" She recoiled, her hand flying to her throat. "Oh, no!"

"Certain matters have gone too far, Kate."

"And you are going to co-operate to the hilt!"

For a moment he was silent, his gaze unwavering before the anguish that was now naked in her white face. Then he gave a hopeless gesture. "Two wrongs never made a right, Kate."

"That's the only way you see it?"

"It's the only way to see it. I'm sorry, Kate."

She watched unbelievingly as he turned away and walked towards the outer door. She took a step forward. "No! Please . . ."

He stopped, not looking at her, and wild impulses made her want to fling herself at him, forcibly to tear the case out of his hand. Then sanity prevailed, and a hopeless acceptance of

146

defeat. She took a deep shuddering breath.

"All right, take it. But if you destroy my parents' happiness through this, I'll hate you for as long as I live!"

"You could be mistaken, Kate," he said very quietly. "I could be saving their future."

"Never!" Kate fought off a wave of weakness that was making the room shimmer. "The only thing you'd ever save is your own ruthless, arrogant, inhuman pride. Your – your stiff-necked sense of duty. Because of that you would risk causing heartbreak in two lives, the two people I love most dearly in the whole world. For that I can never forgive you."

She gripped the edge of the hall table for support, while his features tautened and paled, then shuttered with immobility. "You're wrong, Kate, but I see no point in any more argument." With one glance that stabbed at her like a knife he walked out of the house.

The veranda door slammed, and the telephone began to shrill. Kate moved unsteadily, impelled by the automatic reflex to obey the imperative summons, and felt herself reel. Blackness and light splintered out the room, and a rushing sound came in her ears. She put out her hand, reaching for the wall, the last shred of consciousness still forcing her to get to the phone, and the wall slid upwards under her hand.

For the first time in her life Kate fainted.

\*    \*    \*

She did not know how much time passed, perhaps moments, perhaps hours, while voices sounded and she felt herself being lifted. Everything was hazy and miles away, someone fumbled at her clothing and she was powerless to protest, and a voice said, "Not yet – " and hands closed on each side of her face.

There was a whirring sound, and wafts of cool air, and then light began to come back. She moaned softly, remembering the telephone, and exclaimed in a choked little voice "It's stopped."

"Take it easy." She was pushed back against cushions, held by hard hands on her shoulders, and full consciousness returned. She knew the voice and recognised the hands, and her opening eyes closed in aversion to the face of Brad Sheridan bending over her.

Behind him hovered Benny, a glass in his hands and a scared look on his face. Brad reached for the glass and held it to her lips. "Drink this, Kate."

The liquid was cold, sweet and washed round her mouth with a faintly burning sensation. "What is it?" she asked weakly.

"Water, sugar, and a little brandy. Now lie still for a moment, for heaven's sake." He looked down at her with troubled eyes. "You know what's the matter with you, don't you?"

"I fainted." She took a deep breath, and propped herself on one elbow. "I'm okay now – I never did that before in my life."

"Will you do what you're told, for once in your life," he said impatiently. "It was Mrs. van Hahn on the phone. She's coming over straight away and – " He put up a silencing hand as Kate opened her lips to protest. "Stop worrying! Your parents are being met. Everything's being taken care of. And if you intend making the show tonight you'd be advised to get some food into you and go to bed for the afternoon."

"I can't – I've too much to do. Turn that thing off, please."

He switched off the fan, which was responsible for the cool air and the soft whirring noise which was somehow disturbing to her, then took the glass from her hand. "I've taken the liberty of undoing your bra and waistband," he said acidly. "I thought you may prefer to breathe than remain unconscious. So maybe you'd better not risk standing up."

Before she could frame a reply to this he bent down, thrust his arms under her knees and waist, and picked her up bodily. Something about the iron of those arms and the set of the jaw, grim under its dark shadow of beard not yet shaven, made her stay tense but unresisting as he carried her through into her bedroom. He paused a moment by the bed, and a tremor of fear ran through her as suddenly his repressed anger communicated itself from the indrawn breath that heaved his chest.

"Perhaps Mrs. van Hahn may talk some sense into that stubborn head of yours, Kate. You certainly won't take it from me."

Her retort was stifled by the abruptness with which he all

but threw her down on to the bed, and the bitterness that curled his mouth as he glared at her.

"Don't bother," he gritted curtly. "I've got the message, Kate. I should have got it right at the start."

The next moment he had gone.

The silence seemed to quiver with the angry force of his exit. At last Kate sat up wearily and fought the impulse to bury her head in her hands and weep. With the chill dread of certainty she recognised the finality of Brad Sheridan's parting gesture; she too had got the message. He would never come back.

Well, she didn't want him to! She wanted never to see him again. Kate stood up and went to the mirror, to recoil in horror from the white-faced, distraught girl that stared back from dark-shadowed eyes. Eyes that said: Liar, and a mouth that trembled with unhappiness. Oh, damnation! She turned away furiously and tore off her sweater and slacks. She wasn't going to make a fool of herself over one impossible man; she wasn't going to let herself care!

She snatched up her robe and flung into it; when she'd had something to eat, and a bath, and pulled herself together ... She reached the door as the knock came on its outer panel, and opened it to Lorna van Hahn's anxious gaze.

"Oh, honey!" Lorna took a step back and the anxiety in her face gave way to startled concern. "Whatever happened to you? I've been trying to contact you all morning! And what's all this about a car accident, and your collapsing? Your house-boy didn't know a thing, where you'd got to or anything. And whatever got into our Mr. Sheridan?" she rushed on. "I just met him out there, and he looked like a thundercloud. As though he was going to bite my head off, for daring to ask – "

She paused, seeing the brittle control stretched to breaking point, and put her hands on Kate's shoulders. "I'm sorry – asking all these questions."

"It's true," Kate said wearily. "I – I took the wrong track in the car last night and landed in a swamp. We – we couldn't get back, and I ricked my ankle quite badly, and I don't know how they'll get the car out, and – " she gulped, brushing her hand across her brow, "my parents will be back any minute, and – "

"I know. Now stop worrying. Go and get ready." Lorna's voice took on a briskness Kate recognised. "Leave it to me."

Kate was too tired to argue. Benny arrived at that moment with a tray on which reposed a cup of strong tea, a buttered roll and a plate of biscuits. Lorna took it from him, put it on the bedside table, and said firmly: "Now sit down and drink that—and relax for a few minutes. Like a couple of aspirins?"

"Just the tea." Kate subsided, and to her relief they left her alone.

The strong sweet tea helped to calm her, and she bit into the roll, discovering how very hungry she was as soon as the food touched her lips. A few minutes later, a little more in control of herself, she had a quick shower and slipped into blessedly cool clean clothes. She could hear sounds of brisk activity in the other parts of the bungalow, and guessed that Lorna was organising things. When she emerged from her room, immaculate grooming adding its frail touch of confidence once more, she discovered that Lorna had indeed spent a very busy twenty minutes.

The dining table was beautifully set, silver and glasses gleaming, there were fresh flowers in the sitting room and hall, cushions had been plumped and in the kitchen the salad was tastefully garnished, the wine selected, and the food all ready to bring from the cooling cabinet to the table. Benny stood by, looking slightly apprehensive and somewhat bemused, and Lorna was adding little diamond-shaped pieces of angelica to a chilled cream topping on the fruit salad.

She turned, laughing. "I've raided your reserves – I used an apricot brandy liqueur for this. Okay?"

"It looks wonderful – I'd never have achieved all this in time," Kate said unsteadily. "But you shouldn't . . ."

"And why shouldn't I?" Lorna wiped her hands and unexpectedly turned to kiss Kate lightly on the cheek. "You look lovely – a new girl. Now, I'd better fly – they'll be here any moment."

"Please, stay to lunch." Kate put a hand out to underline the invitation. "I'd like you to meet my mother."

Lorna hesitated, then shook her head. "You don't want a

guest at this special homecoming, honey. But will you invite me again? Promise."

Kate nodded, suddenly realising that Lorna would have a lot of last-minute details to see to back at the hotel, some of which should have been Kate's business.

Lorna's car had scarcely left before the sound of another approached the house. Kate ran to the door and down the veranda steps, and a moment later she was in her mother's embrace.

For a few joyous moments, while John Merrivale stood by, Kate forgot the unpleasant news she would have to break to her father before very long. Somehow she would have to get him alone, but it was very difficult. Mrs. Merrivale was overjoyed to be home and she had so much to tell them and so many messages to relay from old friends she had met during her stay in England.

Lunch became a very extended meal, with Kate and her father inevitably finishing each course first and Mrs. Merrivale suddenly realising that she was talking so much that her food was remaining scarcely touched on her plate. And then over coffee John Merrivale suddenly perceived that his daughter was both strained and unhappy beneath the outward excitement engendered by her mother's return.

He said rather too casually, "Anything happened while I was away, Kate?"

She took a deep breath. "Yes, I've crocked the car."

"What!" His cup clattered on its saucer. "You've – "

"I know – I feel dreadful about it, but – "

"Darling, when?" Mrs. Merrivale went white. She put her hand on her husband's arm to silence him. "Never mind about the car. Kate, you might have been killed! Are you sure you're all right?" She got up and came round to Kate at the other side of the coffee table, sitting beside her and putting an anxious arm round her daughter's shoulders. "How did it happen?"

Almost relieved that she could unload this part of her worry, Kate explained, omitting only the vital reason for her journey. Fortunately her mother did not even think to enquire about this, but Mr. Merrivale was not so easily pacified.

"I wondered why it should be Rex Winton at the airfield to

meet us. But I didn't give a second thought to his vague explanation that you'd got held up." Annoyance clouded Kate's father's face. "What the devil were you doing driving along that ghastly track at that time of night? And what was Brad thinking of to allow it? To let a girl cope with those conditions! What was the matter with his own car if he wanted to take you joy-riding, anyway? Really, I shall – "

"No, it wasn't like that at all!" Kate broke in desperately. "I wanted to drive – I insisted. It was all my fault, and of course I'll pay for the damage to the car." She sent him an imploring look that begged him not to question her further. Her mother had always possessed an infallible instinct for knowing when Kate wasn't being entirely truthful – and one no less acute for sensing when something was wrong.

"The damage to the car is the last thing we'll worry about." Mrs. Merrivale came to Kate's rescue, all her protective maternal instincts to the fore. "What a dreadful experience, darling. And you'll have had no sleep! And I expect you've been rushing round all morning getting this lovely meal ready for us." Kate felt like a fraud, while Mrs. Merrivale's restored keen gaze searched her daughter's face intently and was not reassured by what she saw. "You're going to put your feet up, my pet, or you'll feel thoroughly washed out by tonight, and you want to be at your best for the show."

There was no arguing with Mrs. Merrivale. And no opportunity for Kate to break the other dreadful news to her father in secret. Kate, making anxious confessions about the true maker of the lovely meal, was shepherded firmly to her room and made to lie down with cool moist pads over her eyes and a pillow under her feet, while the venetian blinds were drawn to shut off the blaze of the afternoon sun.

Kate lay there, her body immobile and her mind a turmoil, and heard the to-and-fro of her mother's light steps as she unpacked in the next room. Every so often the wardrobe door clicked softly as Mrs. Merrivale hung up a garment, and then the familiar creak of the third drawer down that always stuck when it was halfway closed. There would be the little gifts from London, waiting in their gay gift paper for Kate's murmurs of delight, and her father's exclamation of pleasure, and the picture postcards Mrs. Merrivale always bought of each place she visited and liked.

The moistened pads on Kate's eyes grew warm, then hot with the force of her unshed tears. If only she weren't so helpless. If only she knew! What was Brad Sheridan doing? Where was Walt Marlow? What was in that briefcase that was so vital to Walt? Kate stirred, her hands clenching with the pent-up frustration she had no way of assuaging. She kept seeing Brad Sheridan's face, hearing his voice, reliving the bitter recrimination of those moments when he had destroyed the last fragile threads of hope and illusion. In her heart she had not really believed that he would remain so totally impervious to her pleas. But he had, and the knowledge racked like the pain of a raw wound. Kate flung the hot dry pads from her eyes and rolled over, working her face deep into the dark softness of the pillow. She might as well be honest and admit what ailed her most of all.

She was in love with Brad Sheridan.

*     *     *

The rest of that day passed in a curious haze of unreality.

Her mother brought her a tray with tea at four-thirty and sat companionably by the bedside while Kate sipped tea and talked of the coming evening as though not a cloud hovered to darken her horizon. Her father had gone out, Mrs. Merrivale was vague as to where, and he did not return until Kate was about to leave for the hotel. Once there, Kate was surrounded by the hectic suspense that always preceded a show, particularly so in this case when so much of the responsibility rested on Kate's own shoulders.

A kind of brittle calm possessed her; she checked final details, calmed poor Lucy, whose rash had almost but not quite disappeared, arbitrated in a threatened squabble between two of the girls, and enthused with Kim, whose oriental inscrutability had given way at last to almost delirious excitement. Several reporters had turned up, one with a photographer from the

Singapore branch of an international news agency, and best of all, someone whom Kate knew very well indeed, the fashion editor of a famous "glossy".

"Aren't we in luck?" enthused Lorna. "Actually she's on holiday – who says the arm of coincidence never stretches! Come and meet her."

Marda Laraine was in the cocktail lounge. She turned an assessing glance on Kate and waved languidly. "So this is where you're hiding, darling. How did you find her?"

"We have a grapevine here too," Kate returned coolly. "I take it you've had a preview."

"This afternoon."

There was no further comment, and Kate, knowing from experience that Marda Laraine would never commit herself until she was ready, made no attempt to probe for reactions. Let Marda see for herself this evening before she passed judgement. Nevertheless, it was a promising omen and Kate's depressed spirits lifted a little. Something told her that in this respect at least, her hopes were to be happily realised.

During the course of that evening Kate broke one rule she had imposed on herself rigidly ever since that tremulous day when she had modelled her very first gown; that was never to look at her audience. But now she sought from under shadowing lids for a discreet glimpse of Marda Laraine, and was not disappointed.

Marda was making notes, lots of them, and once Kate was positive she was making sketches. Kate did not object; Marda might be autocratic and devoid of any sentiment whatever, but she was strictly honest, there would be no poaching of ideas there. If she liked what she saw it could mean the making of Kim in the fashion-design world.

The place was packed, and despite the air-conditioning the heat became stifling. Kate made her own final change, into the glorious blue and silver formal gown, and began her parade. She heard the soft murmurs of acclaim, of admiration from the women and the frank interest of the men present, and withdrew herself into the cool exquisite shell that was simply a lovely body to mould the creation of another mind. In this kind of gown she was untouchable, not quite real, to her audience a being who somehow could not possibly ever suffer the aching frailties of head or limbs which beset lesser mortals, least of all an aching heart.

She began the long glide down the centre catwalk, pausing, turning, to display the gown to full effect, and suddenly out of the blur that was all around her a crystal cameo swam into focus. The rectangle of doorway and columns, the man who was lounging there, one shoulder against the white marble, a twist of blue smoke coiling from a cheroot in his hand. Brad Sheridan inclined his head, his hand moved in an almost imperceptible salute, and she heard his whispered, mocking, "Back where you belong, sweet Kate?"

Her heart gave a choking bound, and only her professional control saved her from stumbling. A pulse throbbed in her throat, but she stared over his head, turned and made the long return to the dais.

It seemed a mile and an eternity, and when she looked again the rectangle of doorway was blank. She was trembling when she reached the dressing room and stood while Madam Kee Lun helped her out of the gown. She hardly heard the applause, and then the outbreak of discussion now that it was all over. Reality invaded any triumphant pleasure her success might have inspired and the wind-up became simply an ordeal to be endured until she was free to face the moment she dreaded. Her smile began to feel as though it was nailed on her face as she circulated and met the many people to whom she was introduced. The evening turned into a gala, with the medley of many tongues. As Lorna had hoped a large contingent were there from the conference, and there were at least thirty different nationalities enjoying the dancing and wining that looked like going on well into the small hours of the next day. Marda Laraine congratulated Kate and promised a feature in her magazine, there were interviews and photographs, and when she belatedly remembered that she should be making sure the clothes were being properly packed in their travelling robes she found herself being drawn aside by Lorna, who wore a conspiratorial expression. In a small side room were Kim and Madam Kee Lun, and in a polythene dress cover was the blue and silver gown, a card and an orchid pinned to one corner.

"Yes, Kate, for you, and all you have done," Kim reached up to kiss her, adding, "I hope I will be able to make many more for you one day."

Madam Kee Lun, less demonstrative, shook her hand gravely, and Lorna removed the orchid and pinned it to the shoulder of the white silk jersey dress Kate was wearing.

They all smiled at her, and Kate felt her throat constrict. It was a magnificent gift, unexpected, and undeserved in her opinion. But they did not agree and Kate followed them out of the little room dangerously near tears. She threaded her way through the crowd, looking for her parents, and she did not notice the group of company personnel gathered at one side, talking in an agitated manner and no trace of their former gaiety left on their shocked faces.

Kate saw her mother at last, sitting with Lena Maddison at the far side of the room. She was halfway across when a hand fell on her shoulder and she whirled round, to see her father. There was no smile, no indulgence on his face, only a blanched look of shock that struck instant fear into her heart. Oblivious of the crowd milling round she gasped: "What is it? You – "

"Kate, for God's sake! Why didn't you tell me?"

"Tell you what?" she whispered, even as she knew beyond doubt what it must be. "What happened?" she faltered.

"It's Walt. He was arrested today, in Penang."

Arrested! Already! Kate swayed, and the shapes of the Chinese lanterns looped overhead misted and receded.

"Why didn't you tell me?" John Merrivale repeated. "It seems to be common knowledge that he vanished from Mahore two days ago. Didn't you know?"

"Yes . . ." Kate strove for control and clutched his arm. "We can't talk here. I wanted to tell you – that was what last night was all about – but there wasn't a chance." She pulled at his arm, steering him in the direction of the ante-room she had left only moments previously. To her relief it was empty. She pushed the door to, and took a deep breath.

"There was a briefcase – Walt phoned me last night. I had

to take it to him, to Bahru, and the car was jibbing, and then Brad Sheridan arrived ..." In jerky, broken phrases she told him, and ended desperately, "I tried to stop him, but he refused to listen. Father, he's got that briefcase! What are we going to do?"

"The stupid young fool!" John Merrivale paced across the floor. "I knew this would happen."

"Father!" she cried. "I don't give a damn what happens to Walt Marlow. He can go to jail until kingdom come, but what about you? It'll break Mother's heart!"

He did not seem to comprehend what she was saying, and she caught at his arm. "For heaven's sake, tell me the truth! How far are you involved in all this? Whatever Walt has done – I know it's fraud to do with the company and that's why Brad Sheridan was sent here – but can he drag you into it?"

John Merrivale gave a start, and his face grew angry. "No, darling, Walt can't drag me into anything. But he had no right to involve you."

"I couldn't do anything else! He blackmailed me into trying to help him! In exactly the same way as he blackmailed you."

When he did not answer, except to stare at her with shock in his eyes, she gave a despairing sigh. "I know, Father. I didn't want to believe it. But everything that has happened all adds up to convince me. How can I go back to England and leave you until it's all cleared up?"

She waited, anguish making a white mask of her lovely oval face, and at last he walked to a chair and sank down heavily.

"I started to suspect, oh, a long time ago, that something was wrong," he began slowly. "I didn't say anything, because I hoped against hope that I was mistaken, but all my discreet inquiries seemed to lead back to Walt. It was so obvious, Katy – his extravagances, his cars, his women, and his gambling. I had a fair idea of what he earned and I knew it couldn't possibly stretch to his style of living. At last I was forced to conclude that he was robbing the firm and I accused him, told him what I believed, and begged him not to make a complete fool of himself. I told him that if he was in such dreadful difficulties I would try to help him, to clear up his debts." John Merrivale paused, and looked away. "It was then that he told me about Leila and threatened to tell Jean everything if I persisted in interfering. He said I had no proof and denied everything. So what could I do? I had no definite proof, and if I had I dared not use it. This was just before Brad Sheridan's arrival. I knew I should have told him of my suspicions, but I tried to square my conscience, telling myself that it was his job, not mine. I had to think of Jean before anything else."

"And you're sure that's all?" she persisted.

"Of course it is!" he shot at her. "For God's sake, Kate, do you really suspect your own father of – of wholesale larceny? I've never taken a penny that didn't belong to me all my life. Nor am I likely to."

Kate was silent. At least that threat was removed. Whatever the briefcase contained surely it could hold no danger for her father. But there was still the other ...

The music drifted to her ears, the slow sweet sensuous melody of *Moon River*, infinitely nostalgic. It recalled the very first time she had danced with Ken Lester, melted in his arms on a dance floor lit with moonlight and every sense responding to the new magic of love ... Now she could think of Ken without a pang, except that of the tender nostalgia of first love. But the music still wrought its alchemy, making imagination create another man in her arms, another man who held the power to weave the eternal irresistible spell of desire ... But Brad Sheridan had abused that power, made her despise him, and despise herself even more for succumbing to its thrall.

Kate closed her heart to traitorous weakness and looked down at her father's bowed head. She touched his shoulder. "Is it true about Leila?" she asked quietly.

He reached up and enclosed her hand. "In a way, Kate. But never the way Walt believes."

"Tell me," she whispered. "For I know enough of life now to understand that these things happen. And also that you would never deliberately deceive my mother or hurt her."

"I didn't want you to know. I'd hoped it was all forgotten," he said wearily. "It was all so long ago. Leila was a very unhappy woman, she'd had a very unhappy girlhood, and she married the first man who asked her, because it seemed the only way of escape. The tragedy of it was that it had to be Matt. I didn't love her, Katy. I could never love any other woman but your mother, but I was sorry for her. Matt, while he was kind and loved her in his fashion, had never got over the loss of his first wife, and he couldn't understand why Leila was so restless and unable to settle down on a remote plantation. And of course he wanted a child – he longed for a daughter and doted on you, as you probably remember."

Kate nodded, her mouth soft with memory of the big kindly man she had known as Uncle Matt. How his son could grow so different in nature and manner from his father was something she had never understood.

"But Leila was terrified of the idea," John Merrivale went on. "She was convinced something would go wrong at the birth and medical help wouldn't get through to her in time, and she flatly refused to take the risk. And then Walt was difficult. At first he resented her, and she hadn't the faintest idea of how to cope with an adolescent stepson. His weekends and holidays from school invariably threw up at least one scene and she was desperate for the time when Walt would be packed off to college. And then suddenly he developed a strange kind of adoration for her. It unnerved Leila, and one day she confided all her troubles to me. I advised her as well as I could, reassured her that Walt would grow out of his teenage rebellions and fantasies. It wasn't until much later, when it was too late, that I realised Leila was becoming attracted to me."

He paused, his eyes shadowed with pain. "Life became a nightmare. Trying to go on as though nothing had changed. The evenings Jean and I spent at the Marlows' place; the evenings they came to us. Mahore was a much smaller town in those days. Only the hotel, a couple of traders, the bank and the little mission. There was no air link then, just the railway and the weekly boat. Everybody knew everybody, and somehow, wherever I went I seemed to encounter Leila, until the day she broke down and said she loved me. Of course I tried to repulse her, as gently as I could, hoping I could laugh her out of it, and she started to weep, begging me to love her and take her away. I couldn't get her to understand that what she suggested was impossible. I could never leave my wife and my little daughter. You and Jean were – still are – my whole world. And Matt was my closest friend."

John Merrivale drew a tremulous breath and looked up at Kate, his eyes pleading for understanding. "But how can a man, unless he's totally devoid of compassion, be brutal to any woman in distress? I had to comfort her, and I think that was the only time I ever held Leila in my arms; and I think Walt saw. Maybe it looked different to him, who knows how it would appear to a boy's eyes? I was only trying to reason with her, begging her not to jeopardise her marriage, and at last I persuaded her to go home and make a determined effort to settle down and be a good wife to Matt. I managed to avoid her the rest of that week, and then Matt had to go on business to Singapore that weekend. As a rule Leila went with him, but this time she stayed at home. He could scarcely have reached town before the houseboy landed over with a note for me, from Leila."

Again Kate's father paused, his eyes haunted by memory.

"I'll never forget that day. The boy standing waiting, while I read Leila's desperate message. She said she'd tried, but she couldn't go on any longer. She was leaving Matt, because she couldn't stay with him the way she felt about me. She said she would wait for me at the hotel. *'Please, my darling. I can't live without you.'* "

He was silent, and Kate's heart went out to him. It needed little imagination to picture the impasse in which he had been caught through no fault of his own. She waited, and he bowed his head.

"I did the only thing I believed right in the circumstances. God alone knows if things might have turned out differently had I obeyed her impassioned plea. But I simply turned the note over and scribbled on the back *'You must know my answer, Leila. Forget this crazy idea,'* and slipped it into an envelope and told the boy to return it to Mrs. Marlow. Then I told Jean I had to visit the northern sector of the plantation, which entailed taking the boat up the river and being away a couple of nights.

I reckoned by the time I got back Matt would be home and Leila would either have come to her senses or gone alone. When I did get back I learned the appalling news."

For a moment he buried his face in his hands, before he looked up at Kate. "I've blamed myself ever since. But how could I know? What should I have done?"

"I don't know," Kate whispered. "I don't know."

"If I'd gone to her at the hotel it would have only ended in another hopeless impasse," he said despairingly, "and I felt that my first duty and loyalty were due to my wife and daughter. So this is the guilt I've lived with all these years. And this is the hold Walt Marlow possesses. The means of breaking my wife's heart."

"No, my dear. Not any longer," said a soft voice from the doorway.

His head jerked up, and Kate whirled violently to see her mother standing there. Jean Merrivale came forward and sat beside the stricken man. "Why did you never tell me all this?"

"And risk destroying our happiness?" he cried vehemently. "No, I could never take that risk, my dear. I couldn't bear the thought of you being hurt."

"But I knew." She took his hand in her own. "I always knew. Poor Leila, she didn't make a very successful job of disguising her feelings where you were concerned. A wife can always sense these things – if she's very much in love with her husband."

"And yet you never once told me of your suspicion?"

She shook her head. "It wasn't suspicion. It was instinct, John. Oh, often I was tempted to," she admitted. "Often I longed to ask you about Leila – because sometimes I felt sure you were blind to what was so obvious to me. Afterwards I wished with all my heart that I had. Perhaps it might have changed the course of tragedy. But I stayed silent," she went on sadly, "because I didn't know how to begin. Because I loved you, and I knew you loved me. And most of all, because I trusted you."

John Merrivale was staring at his wife as though he was seeing her anew for the first time. He gave an incoherent murmur and drew her close against him. Watching them, Kate swallowed hard on the emotion constricting her throat. Suddenly she knew that this was what loving was all about. This was the true meaning of trust.

Jean Merrivale disengaged herself gently from her husband's arms and managed a tremulous smile. She held out her hand to Kate, and looked down at her husband.

"Let's go home," she said simply.

Slowly Kate went to get her wrap and say the goodnights which had to be said, then rejoined her parents. She was conscious of the weakness of relief that fear and unhappiness and suspicion were overcome at last. Walt Marlow, whatever his fate was to be, could never threaten the kind of love that united her parents. He could never touch their lives again, but what of her own?

Kate's tender goodnight to her father and mother at the end of that long momentous day gave no hint of her innermost self, of that strange empty feeling as though part of her had withered and died.

This was something she would have to learn to live with.

# CHAPTER NINE

KATE spent the last week of her stay relaxing quietly with her parents. On her last evening she gave a small informal dinner party, just themselves, Fay, Lorna, the Maddisons, and Rex Winton, on whom everyone had taken pity since Elaine departed for the indulgence of her family and the more equable clime of Melbourne while she awaited the birth of her baby.

Outwardly, the guests gave every indication of enjoying themselves, but despite the façade of bright sociality an air of restraint, almost sadness, hung over the evening. It was the same atmosphere that had tinged the whole week.

"Is it only me? Or has it been a flat week?" Rex gave a wry smile as he voiced the unspoken thought of them all.

"No, we've all got the blues," Fay sighed. "And it's going to be flatter than ever after you've gone." Her glance swung to Kate. "Unless we get some new blood soon there'll be none of us left at this rate."

It was true, Kate thought in the small silence which followed. Lorna was leaving tomorrow, on the same plane as Kate, and Tom Maddison was due for retirement in two months' time. And Brad had gone, the day after the show.

Kate's mind skated warily round the two missing names, but it was proving almost impossible to banish all thought of Brad Sheridan and Walt from her mind. Very few details had filtered through regarding Walt. but this did not prevent several wild rumours circulating in Mahore. Someone said that Walt was actually arrested for starting a punch-up when he was stopped for questioning at Penang Airport. The unfortunate airport official had suffered injuries severe enough to require hospital treatment and the report said that Walt was still in custody awaiting deportation. Another rumour hinted that Mahore Latex had not yet pressed charges, that their investigations were not yet complete. Kate had found herself asked for information; because of her friendship with Lorna van Hahn it was taken for granted that she was bound to be the recipient of inside know-ledge. But Kate would never presume on a new friendship she liked and valued for its own sake, not because of any other advantage it might confer. Besides, she could not find it in her heart to feel much concern for Walt Marlow. He was out of their lives now, and she could feel only relief at the thought. As for Brad . . .

She had fought a long wrangle with conscience and pride that day following the show. Conscience had wondered: shouldn't she, in the light of events, attempt a measure of peace-making before she departed? In the torment of worry she had flung bitter accusations at him, accusations which now proved void. Then pride had hardened her heart. Only chance had proved them so. His arrogant determination could have brought dis-aster, and he had remained totally impervious to her pleas. Pride won, reminding her of all those other times of pain, of the afternoon of the storm at Rainbow Lagoon, the way he had trampled down her defences, made her want his love as she wanted no man's before, but all for his own ruthless purpose. And then her father had come home with the news that the car had been towed out of the mud and was now at the vehicle repair station. She knew that they had Brad to thank for organising the rescue, and again her resolve had wavered. But too late. Her father had added the news that Brad was leaving that evening.

She had not really believed it when the few hours had slipped by, and then the time of the plane's departure. The bungalow where Brad had stayed was less than a hundred yards from the Merrivales', and he had chosen not to cross that short distance to say goodbye . . .

But why should he? Kate asked herself fiercely. She was being both stupid and illogical. She had made her personal feelings quite clear as far as he was concerned, hadn't she? And Brad himself had dispelled any doubts about that.

"*I've got the message*," he had told her.

Kate jolted back to the present with the guilty realisation that someone was speaking to her and her mother was giving her a discreet, reproachful nudge. She responded with an apology and went to get the book she had promised to give Lena some time ago.

The party was breaking up now, with the inevitable lingerings of guests who could never manage to make a brisk and final adieu. The Maddisons were a bit like that, always remembering the most important things they wanted to say just as they reached the doorstep, but they were sweet and homely, Kate thought affectionately. Fay, as usual, was looking for a lift, and Rex Winton smiled.

"I'll take you home, Fay," he offered, then added, "If you promise not to tell Elaine!"

There was laughter, and a general pact of promise. Fay giggled archly. "I promise not to seduce you, darling." There was more laughter, and she added wryly: "I guess I'm missing Brad."

"Oh!" Tom Maddison gave her a sly glance. "May we ask why? Or is it an indiscreet question?"

"Not at all." Fay adjusted a film of electric blue chiffon over her blonde curls. "He often gave me a lift back from the club. And don't look at me like that! It was strictly platonic – worse luck!"

"Another one!" Lorna smiled at Kate. "That young man seems to have made an impact on Mahore in more ways than one."

"We'll get up a petition and have him transferred back for you," Rex said flippantly.

"It's strange that you should say that." Fay gave a knowing smile. "That might just happen – from what he told me."

*What had he told Fay?* Instantly a traitorous desire urged Kate to prompt Fay to further confidence, but she made herself stay silent, until Lena provided the cue of curiosity.

"Yes, he might be coming back permanently," said Fay. "And he's thinking of buying a house by the lagoon. Anyone remember a Dr. Lim?"

"Yes," said Kate's father, "I do."

"He used to run the clinic there, before the new hospital was built, then he went to K.L. I didn't know that white house you can see on the other side belonged to him. It's called Mas

Pasir. Anyway," Fay patently was not greatly interested in the house's owner, "Brad knows him, and apparently Dr. Lim has decided to sell it and retire to the east coast instead. I do hope Brad does come back."

There were vague murmurs of agreement, and Kate hoped her fixed smile was hiding the turmoil of emotion that Fay's sudden disclosure had aroused. Brad ... in the white villa ... by the little beach ...

The ache and the knowledge cried in her heart as she smiled her farewells and endured the spate of good luck sentiments as they departed. The ache and the disillusion were still there when the final moment of parting came at the airport the following day.

Her mother was very near tears. "Oh, Katy, I wish you weren't going."

Kate held her tremulously, holding desperately to her own shaky control. "Cheer up," she whispered. "Goodbyes are always the worst part – but it isn't for ever, you know, darling."

Mrs. Merrivale nodded, unconvinced. "It seems so crazy now I think of it, you being over here while I was over there, and then ... having so little time together."

"But somebody had to look after our number one man – he's the only one we have." Kate kept her voice light, knowing if she didn't her mother would break down. "Anyway, you know perfectly well that before I've been gone five minutes you two will have had your little sigh and then settled down like a pair of old lovebirds."

"We can't wait!" John Merrivale put his arm round his still slender, attractive little wife and pulled her close. "And not so much of the old!"

Lorna van Hahn, who had tactfully drawn aside for a little while, now judged it the moment to make her own farewells to Kate's parents. "*My* husband always seems to be too busy to see me off," she grumbled wryly as at last they turned to board the plane.

A few minutes later they were airborne. Mahore fell away below and the dense green slopes threaded by the brown swirling ribbon of river stretched into the distance like a thick rumpled carpet running down to the sea. Kate watched, picking out the landmarks she knew before they skimmed away beneath, and wondered how long it would be until she saw them again.

She had a break of several hours to while away before her major flight that evening from Singapore. Lorna suggested a light meal, and then there was time for a visit to Madam Kee Lun and Kim.

They found Kim in a somewhat subdued mood.

"She expects everything to happen like that!" Her mother snapped her fingers and looked appealingly at Kate. "Perhaps if you tell her, she will believe that everything takes its allotted time – if it's destined to happen at all."

Kim looked a bit happier after Kate and Lorna had assured her that they had every confidence in it all happening for Kim if only she would be patient just a little while longer. However, despite her impatience, Kim had not wasted her time since her return from Mahore. She had completed another batch of designs, and these Kate decided to take back with her to show to contacts in the London fashion world who she was certain would be interested. Kim had also begun a scrapbook. Only the first page was filled, it was true, but Kate was sure it wouldn't be very long before there were many more press cuttings to add to the two proudly pasted there alongside two news pictures from the local press.

Lorna smiled over the two pictures, one which included Kate and herself in the group against the familiar background of the hotel, but Kate stared at the other one, her heart giving the sudden sharp pang she was learning to expect at every reminder of Brad Sheridan. Even in the blurred and shadowy background behind Kim he was instantly recognisable. He had obviously been unaware of the cameraman, but the flash had caught his profile and the outline of his broad shoulders as he talked to Fay Slessor.

"I have ordered proper copies, big ones, from the newspaper office," Kim was saying excitedly. "Would you like me to send them to you when they come?"

Kate nodded, her mouth smiling but her eyes sad. It was all she was likely to have for her own scrapbook of memories ...

With the bitterness of self-knowledge she knew she was jealous even of Fay, because a few seconds of pure chance had bound the lonely young widow and one certain man for ever together in the grey tones of a newspaper photograph. And he had told Fay about his plans for the future, careless confidences he had never made to Kate ... How little she knew of him ... and how little of the foolish weakness of herself. Desperately she told herself that it was simply an episode, he was an attractive man with a potent sex appeal few women would resist. She certainly wasn't the first, and she wouldn't be the last. Once she was back in London, among her friends, with loads of work to occupy her days and sublimate her energy these few short months would fade back in time, assume their rightful proportion in the pattern of her life. She would look back and smile at her intensity of emotion, see it as the infatuation it really was ...

Kate was still trying to convince herself when she boarded the 707 that evening, and settled down for the long flight into the darkness. But now she was alone, and the memories were difficult to keep at bay. Dinner was served almost as soon as they were airborne, but Kate's appetite was nil; eating was only a means of pretence, a spinning out of the time until the first stop at Bahrein, trying not to imagine a house that over-looked a beach fringed with feathery casuarinas, her childhood dream paradise with a name to evoke the senses – or fill a heart with hopeless longing.

She stepped down from the plane into the dismal grey chill of a late November morning. Her flat felt equally chill and unwelcoming, although her landlady had switched on the storage heaters the previous day, left milk and bread for her, and put the accumulation of mail in a neat pile on the table. Kate unpacked and sorted out more suitable clothing to combat Britain's own particular mixture of drizzle and mist and raw cold, then spent the rest of the morning in a shopping foray to replenish her larder. It was always like this the first day back, she told herself, still determined not to give in to the numb, drained feeling that persisted in sapping her vitality. The shops were ablaze with light and tinsel and holly and glittering baubles – all the commercial trappings of the festive season. Kate's spirits ebbed even lower; she had never felt less like Christmas.

But those first two weeks were the worst. By the end of them she had picked up most of the threads of her own particular scene and worked back into the routine of her career. She spent a day itching in particularly hairy tweeds for a certain exclusive mill; she wafted in clouds of fragrance at the launching of a new perfume; she shivered on a barrow at crack of dawn at the fruit market for somebody's new pick-you-up beverage that would sustain you anywhere – it sustained Kate much less than a mug of well stewed tea and the rich, good-natured badinage of the market porters and drivers who were unabashed by the invasion of cameras and models. She was informed by her bitchiest best friend of two new arrivals on the model scene who were about to relegate Kate and her contemporaries to last decade's has-beens. Her bank sent her a statement to remind her of her depleted resources, which was not at all pleasant, Bart squired her to a lush reunion night out, which was, and she met a new man. Jeremy was good-looking, charming, and wealthy. He assumed a masterful, proprietorial attitude, left her emotions completely uninvolved, but resuscitated her damaged pride which was what she needed most of all – except the cure she couldn't have.

Christmas came and went, bringing its quota of cards with exotic eastern stamps, and one from Lorna van Hahn that in a few moments shattered all her hard won shell of composure. Two lines of the note in it instantly projected themselves off the page. "... *by the way, Brad spent a long weekend with us recently. He's got his new house, and he's going to take charge of our technology department from next month ... Kim has good news, but I know she's writing to you herself, so I won't anticipate ...*"

For a little while Kate gave in to the bitter mood of retrospect, even as she knew the foolishness of allowing her imagination to drift into the old blind alley of wishing ... if only ... if only things could have been different ... And then she tried to assuage the reawakened ache by accepting the invitation she had intended refusing. Because it wasn't fair to Jeremy to let him gain the impression that their friendship could ever become anything more than just that – a friendship.

She spent New Year with him at his parents' home in Sussex, and experienced ironic relief when the proposal she was half expecting turned out to be a slightly different proposition altogether.

"But why not, Kate?" Jeremy had the easy persuasiveness born of wealth and what Kate suspected to be the success of several previous similar propositions. "It's the only sensible thing to do. After all, if we prove to be incompatible it'll be far easier to deal with the matter in a civilised manner – not that for a moment I believe we would. And you could see how things worked out in respect of your career. Naturally, I understand that you'd feel reluctant to give it up altogether. And then after, say six months . . ."

Kate disengaged herself from his arms and shook her head with a finality anyone who knew her better would have recognised. "No, Jeremy. I don't believe in trial marriages, even with a ring dangling at the end of six months."

"But I thought . . ." He frowned with sheer disbelief.

She eyed him coolly. "You thought because I happen to be a model I change my men as easily as I change my clothes. You're mistaken. It's a demanding job, and most of us have worked very hard for any success we achieve."

"Kate, you surprise me. My mother was right about you, after all."

"I surprise myself sometimes," she returned calmly. "Your mother, whom I've enjoyed meeting and like very much, is rather more discerning than you give her credit for."

His brows came together. "I don't think I understand."

"There isn't much *to* understand." Sadness touched her mouth and made her smile a bit one-sided. "Write me off, Jeremy, as a very old-fashioned girl who still believes in love – and marriage."

"The happy ever after bit? Oh, Kate!" He was almost laughing with derision. "I don't believe it."

"It happens to be true."

Suddenly his expression changed, to suspicion. He caught her by the shoulders. "Kate, have you been misleading me?

Is there someone else? Another man you – "

"No!" She pulled away. "There's nobody else."

"But I think there is." He moved, determined to see her averted face. "I can tell, just by the way you look."

She sighed, and made no further attempt at evasion, meeting his accusing gaze steadily. "Tell me, would you call a man, who is at the other side of the world, who has no intention of seeing me again, and whom I've no intention of ever seeing again, somebody else?"

Jeremy stared, not answering, and she said bitterly: "If you agree that that constitutes your definition of somebody else, then it's certainly true. There's another man. And there always will be."

Kate felt miserable and guilty for days after her return to town, even though she knew she had been scrupulously careful not to give Jeremy any romantic encouragement during the three brief weeks she had known him. If only she hadn't weakened and accepted his invitation for the holiday; but surely the old seal on a relationship, that of being taken home to meet the family, was outmoded now. It wasn't as though he had made the kind of proposal that his invitation would have presaged in a bygone age, she thought hopelessly.

Suddenly Kate knew there was only one way to deal with this restless, bitter despondency; work and more work, preferably out of the country. She went to see Bart and begged him to find her more foreign assignments.

"What's the matter?" Bart's grin was knowing. "Jeremy getting too eager?"

"No, it isn't Jeremy," she sighed. "It's me."

"Goes a bit further back than Jeremy, doesn't it?" Bart's shrewd eyes had summed up too many girls down the years for Kate to try to dissemble. He always knew. He pinched his nose thoughtfully. "Now where can we send you to sublimate? Not out East for a while, eh?"

Kate coloured. "Anywhere. Anything." She glanced down at the proof of a holiday brochure layout on his desk. "Anything like this?"

"Oh, Katy, Katy!" He pretended shock. "You know you're

not the earthy, sea-and-sand type. Didn't I spend months building your image into the dark, untouchable beauty with mystery – that men can't wait to get their hands on to discover the secret? And I'm beginning to suspect that one man did. Who is he? I'll kill him."

"You won't need to." Kate tried to shut out the fatal memory of a storm-tossed beach by a lagoon ... "What about U.C.?"

"There's still a hold-up." Bart leaned back in his chair and regarded her with worried eyes. "The technical spread got away okay, and I told you I had to send Jenny to Finland – when I didn't get your date of return in time I couldn't hold back any longer. But God knows when we'll get the go-ahead for the miracle fabric. It's so top secret even I can't get any info myself, and until they sort out this hold-up over the trademark – the name they want to use is already registered in France by another manufacturer of a totally different product, which means they'd have to market there under another name – U.C. were very hurt about this – so until then we're stymied. Of course I've started work on provisional layouts, as far as I can go."

"Do you believe this wonder synthetic is really impervious to dirt and stains?" she asked. "I can't imagine a garment that doesn't need cleaning or washing, if only from a personal freshness point of view."

Bart shrugged. "They claim their special built-in factor covers that problem as well. You simply hang the thing up to air for a few hours and any creases fall out and any marks just brush off. I believe the major headache at the moment is the dyeing problem, like terylene and nylon back in the forties. It took a lot of research to overcome the difficulty of deep colour dyeing." Bart stood up. "However, that's not our pigeon, thank heaven. We've only to sell it to the public. Come on, I'll take you for a drink and we'll discuss your future."

Bart was as good as his word. The next two months were very busy indeed for Kate. She did a promotion tour of the capitals of Europe for Amorette, a new range of toiletries. February came in with a particularly foul spell of weather, which Kate escaped during a modelling session in Morocco.

She met the first delicate touch of spring in Paris, and March found her in Jamaica.

This was a rather special assignment, also for a famous manufacturer of synthetics, U.C.'s principal rivals, and she was working with Hillary Peters, one of her favourite photographers, and Simon Devine.

It was the first time she had worked with Simon, and after the first two days of disharmony she was fervently hoping it would be the last.

Simon was a top male model in his own right, and he disliked having to yield even the minutest ray of limelight. He was petty and arrogant, and at times extremely objectionable. These were the moments when his slight lisp became quite pronounced, but even his most arrant detractors could not deny that he was one of the most photogenic models in Europe, and that he stood on the printed page like a rugged, rough-haired twentieth-century Adonis.

He was grumbling now as they reached the secluded little beach Hillary had chosen for their location. "Not again!" he exclaimed, viewing the well-used palm that overhung the beach at an acute angle, almost dipping its fronds into the crystal water. "Not that one, darling. It's famous! Can't somebody think of something *original* for a change?"

"It's the treatment that matters," Hillary said, unmoved by this plea, and began to outline what he wanted. Lindy, the make-up girl, held a mirror for Kate's last-minute inspection, while Simon scrambled up the leaning palm and sat astride its despised bole as Hillary directed.

Simon waited impatiently as Kate followed and Hillary frowned at the huge straw hat she was to wear or hold.

"No, it won't do." The man who was known as Genuis Puck in the camera world took the hat and tried to bend the brim into a shape more pleasing to him. "Try that."

But it still wasn't right, and now Kate's hair was disturbed. Lindy hurried up with a comb, and Simon lost patience.

"For God's sake hurry up," he cried pettishly. "You just want to try sitting here and doing yourself an injury."

"What about me?" Kate retorted. "I have to recline on the

lousy thing."

At last she was arranged to Hillary's satisfaction. "If you could just let your arm hang down, darling – that's fine." He backed away, then, "Damn! That skirt's caught – just ease up a sec, lovey . . ."

She was wearing a full-length beach skirt of white, peppered with huge red and black berries, and a scarlet halter top that left bare a big vee of midriff. The skirt was slit to her thighs, and automatically she raised one knee, stretching the other shapely limb straight down the slanting bole. The hat dangled from her hand, and the full folds of the skirt fell into a flowing drape that almost touched the sand beneath. Hillary was silent at last, and Kate drew a deep breath, praying that no hint of the discomfort and effort entailed in avoiding rolling off her precarious perch would show in the languid, sun-kissed face she turned ready for Hillary's camera.

"Look up . . . down . . . crook leg more . . . close your eyes . . . look down at her Simon . . . smile. . . put the hat over your knee, Kate . . . turn your head a little . . . Simon, put the hat over her face . . ."

"With pleasure, sweetie!" whispered Simon maliciously.

"Throw it up in the air . . . laugh, Kate . . . stretch your arms . . ." Hillary capered, never still, angling, frowning, chiding approving, directing . . "Now, Simon, bend over her. Serious, Kate. Yearn up to him. *Yearn*, darling."

"She doesn't know how to!"

Hillary stopped, and glared round. Simon muttered, "What the hell . . . ?" And Kate all but fell off her uncomfortable support.

She must have dreamed it. That deep, ironic voice. That unmistakeable voice. But Hillary couldn't have dreamed it – and judging by Simon's language he hadn't imagined the interruption.

"Who the devil are you?" Simon glowered at the tall man who had walked up to them unheard, and Kate whispered unbelievingly: *"Brad!"*

Hillary recovered first, and a smile of sheer delight transformed his puckish features. "Oh, perfect! *Lovely*, Katy! Hold it – yes, sit up. That's gorgeous!"

Brad strolled across the pearl-lustre sand and ignoring Simon's furious exclamation reached up to Kate. He put his hands round her waist and lifted her up, holding her aloft for a moment before he allowed her slender weight to slip down against him. When her toes touched the ground he looked into her astonished face with enigmatic eyes.

"You know I'm the only man who can make you yearn," he said softly.

Kate leaned weakly against him. Her eyes glowed, her bones felt like milk, and her spirit had fled to lose itself in a limbo unknown. She knew only that the world had become a wondrous place.

"Well, really!" Simon observed with a glower.

No one took any notice of him. Hillary was too busy with his camera, Lindy was frankly watching this new development, and Simon's indignant gaze ranged over them all with growing incredulity. At last he spluttered:

"Hil, are you quite mad, lover? I'll admit it's a touching reunion, but I mean . . ."

Brad bent his head and kissed Kate with a slow, searching deliberation that completed the defeat of body and soul. Hillary gave a joyous chuckle and prayed the film would last out, and Lindy gave a little sigh.

"They'll slay you for this, Hil," shouted Simon. "You know what a lot of old women they are at Dreamsilk. They get the vapours at the first sniff of permissiveness."

"This isn't for Dreamsilk," Hillary said absently.

"But the togs . . . Oh, well, if nobody's bothered . . ." Simon swung his legs to the ground and stalked away with a petulant swing of his shoulders.

The movement broke the spell at last, and Kate saw sky and sea and palms reform their molecules into an ordered universe. She drew back reluctantly, beginning to realise she had gone more than slightly berserk during the past few minutes.

"Your mother sends her love," Brad was saying, "and did you know you'd left your jade ear-rings behind?"

"Yes – no – I thought I'd lost them. But this is a surprise," she said unsteadily.

"It's a bit late for the surprise act, sweet Kate." The old sardonic humour glinted like twin rapier points in his eyes. "To be truthful, the welcome was more than I dared expect."

Kate wondered if the tumultuous activity of her pulses was actually showing like miniature pounding hammers beneath her satin-tanned skin at wrists and throat. She managed to laugh lightly. "Simon's greeting could scarcely pass as a welcome, I'm afraid. Come and meet Hil. He loves the unexpected subject."

"If it's a natural." Hillary made his mocking little bow.

"My fees are high," Brad warned, above a not unfriendly handshake. "But in this case I'll waive them to compensate for the session I seem to have wrecked."

"I guess I'll call that a deal. Come, children, it's time for refreshments." Hillary donned his large, white-framed sunglasses and indicated the path back to the station wagon.

A state of bemusement had settled on Kate. During the short drive back to the hotel and the convivial session that followed, during which Simon was wooed out of his pet and decided to display his party charm, Kate had the curious sensation of being outside herself, watching a raven-haired girl in a rose-flowered dress and a tall man in the narrowest of white pants and a green and tan beachcomber shirt; watching them looking at one another over the old invisible barrier of wariness that minute by minute was growing as solid as ever it had been.

"Where are you staying?" she asked politely.

"Here."

"Here!"

Brad lifted his glass and eyed her over the rim of it. "This hotel is open to the public, my dear Kate."

Hillary chuckled. "Nor is it reserved for the antics of model boys and girls and their tame cameraman." He drained the last of his lager and sighed gustily. "I was burning up for that."

"Have another," said Brad.

Hillary shook his head. "I'm burning up for a swim now. Come on, Simon – I can see that little dark number by the pool, just yearning for a glimpse of your torso."

Simon yawned and got to his feet. "The boss man he calleth

– can you bear to see me go, lover?"

Kate flashed him a false smile. "The need of your adoring public is greater than mine. See you this evening."

Simon ambled away, and Brad watched him go, his silence expressive. Then he turned back to Kate. "Well?"

"Well what?"

"Let's find a more secluded spot."

Kate stood up and smoothed down her skirt with hands that had suddenly become unsteady. The spate of questions she longed to ask were buzzing round in her head, but she fought to keep them unasked, even though she ached to burst out with why, how, why ... His advent had been a delirious shock, but she dared not unleash the soaring temptation of hope.

Brad put a hand under her elbow, guiding her towards the old stone steps that led from the terrace down to the beach garden. When her feet crunched into the white shingle path she endeavoured to draw away from his infinitely disturbing nearness and pretended an absorbing interest in a vivid abundance of scarlet poinsettias tumbling from a huge mossy urn.

"Someone gave me one at Christmas and all the leaves fell off it," she sighed. "Yet just look at those."

"I didn't follow you here to discuss the cultivation of poinsettias," Brad said in a clipped voice.

"You followed me?" Kate avoided his eyes. "How did you know I was here?"

"By shocking your mother at the cost of the biggest cable bill I or she ever had."

"I hope you're not going to send it to me."

"You've certainly moved around the past few weeks, my girl," he observed with a certain feeling. "Paris. Rome. Bonn. Amsterdam. Tangier. Rabat."

"You've missed one. Copenhagen."

*"Kate!"*

She gave a hasty exclamation and moved on quickly. "I'm sorry, but I never got any of those cables."

"Of course you didn't. I got your mother to contact your aunt and pre-pay her full reply as to your whereabouts."

"What?" At last Kate was shaken out of control. "When did

you see my mother? And how did you know about the ear-rings, anyway?"

"I spent last weekend with your parents, before I flew here," he said coolly.

"You did?" Kate was almost speechless.

"Oh, yes. I felt like one of the family, in fact. I quite enjoyed sleeping in your bed."

"In *my* – ! You slept in my room?"

"You surely didn't expect me to sleep on the veranda?"

Kate was beyond speech by now.

"I thought of you all night."

Kate felt hot, cold, weak, angry and shaken all at once. "And nobody told me! Who do you think you are? All three bears rolled into one?" she cried bitterly. "I hope you had night-mares!"

"No, the thought of you never gave me nightmares, Kate, although I have to admit my dreams were not exactly satis-factory."

"You certainly made yourself at home!"

"Your parents made me very welcome."

"Meaning I didn't?"

"Exactly." Brad reached up to hold back an overhanging branch of creeper. "What are you going to do about it?"

"What do you expect me to do about it?" She made to duck under his arm.

"This." His arm snapped down like a barrier. "I've had about as much as I can take of your particular brand of hos-tility."

"Then why are you here?" She found another barrier at her back and the branch he had yanked down effectively trapping her. "You didn't have to follow me here."

"I came because I want an answer, and I'm not letting you go until I get it," he said grimly.

She looked round desperately, and he closed hard hands on her shoulders. "I never did like taking no for an answer, Kate," he added in the same relentless tone, "and I've no intention of taking it now."

"Is there anything to answer?" She looked up into his

implacable features. "Or anything to gain from it?"

"Yes – the satisfaction of breaking down once and for all that infernal built-in barrier you retreat behind the moment I try to get near you. I want to know why, Kate. Why?"

"You're hurting me!"

The grip of his hands did not slacken one iota. If anything they tightened their bruising grip. Between tight lips he jerked: "I'll hurt you some more if you don't stop tormenting me as well as yourself with evasions."

She put her hands against his chest. "You're crazy! Let me go!"

"Not until I get a straight answer. Why do you deny me?" His eyes burned down into hers, as though they would reach into her soul. "Why do you deny your own feelings as well as mine?"

"I don't!"

"You'll never convince me otherwise. You want me as much as I want you." He was almost shaking her. "Admit it!"

"Never! Oh, won't you leave me alone!"

Her thrusting hands felt the heave of his indrawn breath under them, and then he dragged her hard against him, bending her body into a helpless curve as he fought to her mouth. A passion of anger and frustration burst through all control and made his kiss a bruising onslaught of demand. Kate was held prisoner in the steely, merciless strength of his arms while the heat of his body burned into her as though it would melt every vestige of her resistance, and his kiss seemed to go on into eternity. Kate felt her senses ebb away, and she gasped as he broke the kiss and buried his mouth against her throat. A groan escaped him and his hands moved convulsively over her back.

"How can I ever break through to you?" His mouth roved with fierce desperation under the disorder of satiny dark hair. "Why does every approach, every invitation, every attempt to get through to you end in fiasco? Why do you hate me yet respond to me at the same time?"

He raised his head and at last the demanding possession of his arms slackened and he held her away from him, searching her distraught face with dark ravaged eyes. "What is it, Kate?" he took an unsteady breath, "surely you must know by now."

Kate's lips moved but no sound came from them, save a choked little moan. She had no strength left to fight, no words to parry the remorseless questions to which no answer remained but the truth. Suddenly her body felt drained of all emotion except that of defeat, and the dark silhouettes of the palms blurred against the brilliance of the blue Caribbean sky as her eyes stung with unshed tears. She shuddered, turning her head to hide their betrayal, and heard Brad give a murmur of incredulity.

"Oh, no ... not ... Kate, don't ..." He cradled her shaking body into the curve of one arm and cupped his hand under the averted chin, tilting it up. "Not for me – do I hurt you as much as that?" he whispered raggedly. He stretched a long brown finger up her cheek and touched the crystal drops that glistened along the dark lashes. With unbelievable gentleness he bent to brush his mouth against each closed eye in turn before he pressed her face into his shoulder and tangled his hand in her hair. "Oh, Kate," he whispered at last, "what do I have to do to win your love, and your respect?"

The abrupt swing to tenderness broke the last thread of Kate's resistance. His touch, his arms, his nearness were all more than she could bear. With a convulsive gesture of defeat she turned blindly into his arms and yielded against him with the submission of heartbreak. Her arms went round him and at last she knew the ecstasy and the agony of surrendering to the force of her own desperate longing. "Didn't you know?" she whispered brokenly. "You've won right from the start. Oh, why did you ever come back?"

There was a moment of eternity, then he murmured, "Because I couldn't go on without you, my darling."

*My darling!* The words trembled through her and she wondered if she had imagined the low, husky cadences. She stirred, to look up at him from tear-misted eyes. "Brad, do you ... do you mean – "

"Just what I say. Oh, Kate, you've driven me crazy these past three months, longing for you, wanting you, until I couldn't go on any longer. I had to see you again."

She shook her head, still not daring to believe, and put her hand on the side of his face. "You ... you love me ... ?"

"Love you?" The tension along his jaw whitened his skin. "Oh, God, how I love you! You'll never know how much, you infuriating, secretive girl!"

The sky seemed to blaze and the world felt as though it lurched under her feet. Kate stared up at him with wild, brilliant eyes, and found she was laughing and crying at the same time. "You – I – "

"Will you answer me?" The barely suppressed violence of emotion thickened his voice again. "Why?"

"Why? Why didn't you tell me – you infuriating, secretive man? Oh, Brad!" She was trembling with weakness and triumph and joy. "Oh, Brad, if only you'd given me some hope, if you'd – "

"Given you some hope!" He shut his eyes despairingly. "What about me? Oh, for heaven's sake ..." With a smothered exclamation he put an end to all argument in a way Kate concurred with in full, heartfelt response.

Long minutes later Brad drew away and said unevenly: "Maybe we'd better walk a while – unless you want me to seduce you here and now. And you've still some explaining to do," he added threateningly.

"I'm not the only one!" There was a glowing pink radiance in Kate's cheeks as she reluctantly took heed of Brad's not entirely jocular warning and withdrew from his arms. She stood for a moment, trying to finger-comb her tresses out of the havoc he had made of them, while he waited, his gaze rapt on her with a dark hunger still unappeased in its depth.

He held up that same branch for her to pass beneath, and the fleeting thought passed through her mind: only a brief space since he had enacted that very same thing, yet in that space her whole world had been transformed. She looked up at him as she ducked under his arm, her lips forming a sweet wordless "I love you", and then abruptly she sobered.

"I have to be honest," she said in a low voice. "I thought your interest in me was for two reasons only. To get any information I might have concerning Walt Marlow, and ..."

"And?"

Her shoulders moved slightly under his embracing arm. "I thought you wanted me simply for a transient affair."

"A transient affair! Oh, Kate!" his hand tightened momentarily on her shoulder. "I want you for the rest of my life. But you never gave me a chance to get close to you. Oh, I don't mean physically close. I mean that closeness of trust, the kind of closeness in which each has utter confidence in the other. You see, I knew you were worried, desperately worried, and I was pretty sure you were scared, but I didn't dare take you fully into my confidence until I knew for certain how deeply involved you were with Marlow. And I'll admit you had me puzzled. My first impression was that you were totally indifferent to him, in fact disliked him, and then suddenly you changed. As time went on I began to imagine all kinds of things, horrors, that your two families had earmarked you and Walt for one another."

"Oh, no!" Kate breathed.

"Maybe it seems crazy now," Brad went on, "but you were always so cool, so remote, I never knew what you were thinking, even on the one occasion when I tried to make love to you that day by the lagoon. I was all set for a showdown that day, to ask you to marry me, but it didn't turn out that way. I guess I forgot myself and tried to rush you ..."

Kate stayed silent. She remembered that day as vividly as though it were yesterday, but she would never remind Brad of the dark suspicion which had been born then; it was enough that she had hurled the dreadful accusation at him.

He said slowly, "I suppose, looking back, it must have seemed as though I was always asking questions, but by then I was becoming suspicious of Marlow, and shortly after that you and he seemed to be right on the same scene everywhere. It wasn't until Lena Maddison made a chance remark one day that I began to suspect the real truth."

Kate looked up sharply. "What? What did Lena tell you?"

"Oh, nothing about you and Walt. It was at the club one night ... Tom had been reminiscing about his early days in Malaya, and when he stopped there was one of those sort of nostalgic silences, then Lena said: 'I wonder if there was anything in that talk about Leila and John.'"

Kate stiffened and turned, but Brad was looking straight ahead. He went on, "The name didn't mean anything to me, but I noticed Tom give his wife a warning look, and she said, 'Oh, Brad's discreet enough,' then she told me about Leila's accident and the rumour about her being involved with another man, and that the man was your father. But because everyone liked and respected your father they didn't really believe it was true and they kept quiet about it. Then Tom Maddison said he'd always felt sure that Marlow himself had fabricated the unpleasant rumour."

"No," Kate sighed and looked down at the loose shell-shingle that crunched underfoot, "there was some foundation for it . . ." Steadily she related the whole story to Brad, exactly as her father had told her the night of the show, and concluded with an account of the night Walt had driven her to P'bhamg Batee to shock her with his dreadful accusation and threats.

"I knew it," Brad said grimly. "I'd been inclined to dismiss it after Lena mentioned it as an old evil best forgotten, but it kept coming back to haunt me. I wondered if it *had* been forgotten. Right from the start I had a feeling that Marlow had some kind of a hold over your father and he was using it to involve you as well. The more I thought about it the more convinced I became that Marlow was the troublemaker in all ways. How I wish . . . The thought of that – that chiselling scab hooking you into his power makes my gall rise. But you flatly refused to confide in me and I couldn't ask you point blank. I mean, how could a man ask a girl – the girl he's in love with – if she and her father are being blackmailed because her father had once got involved with another woman, a woman who had committed suicide? You would have been furious, and rightly so. You disliked me quite enough as it was," he added with feeling.

"I don't think I ever disliked you," she confessed slowly. "I was afraid of you. Because I didn't know then what was wrong, only that something was very wrong."

Brad tightened his arm about her, and for a little while they walked on in silence until they reached the point where the gardens ended and the path sloped down to lose itself in the silver beach. A little way along there was a grove of palms and a clearing scooped out under their shade. Here Brad stopped. "There's something I must tell you – some day you may wish to tell your father. I made some enquiries while I was in Singapore, to see if I could discover anything about poor Leila Denton. It wasn't easy, it all happened so long ago, but eventually I met an elderly missionary who had known her and her family in the days before she married Walt's father. What he told me bears out everything you've told me. She was a victim of a deprived childhood and an unhappy home, and this makes it difficult to blame her for anything. But she did almost break up another marriage, when she was scarcely sixteen. She went to work for a young planter, helping his wife with their two children. Leila promptly fell in love with the young man and succeeded in attracting him. The wife found out and after a stormy scene walked out, taking the children with her. Of course the man came to his senses and there was a reconciliation, and Leila had to go. She returned to Singapore, where she had one affair after another until she met Walt's father two years later. I don't think Leila could help herself," Brad sighed. "She had longed all her life for a happiness fate seemed determined not to give her. Undoubtedly it had made her unstable, and to become a second wife, where the previous marriage had been ideally happy, by all accounts, didn't help. It was a dreadful tragedy, but I don't think your father could be blamed for what happened."

Kate nodded, her eyes touched with the sadness that could still reach down the years, for the beautiful girl with the engaging *gamin* smile who had once given a child a gaudy flacon of scent . . .

She looked out to the deep blue horizon. "Have you heard anything about Walt?"

"Walt?" Brad's voice sharpened. "You've no pangs for him, surely?"

"I – I just wondered."

"I doubt if Walt will trouble you or your father any more," was the gim response. "I guessed you were going to him that night, that's why I latched on to you. Not because I wanted that

184

infernal briefcase — we'd already found out all we needed — but I wanted to protect you."

"You knew all the time?"

"There are very few tricks that have never been tried," Brad said ironically, "but Walt certainly managed to work some of them for years. The phantom tappers on the pay roll. The crooked ledgers. Always managing to keep one step ahead when anyone raised a question, like your father did."

"My father told you of his suspicions?"

"Yes."

"I'm glad," she said thankfully. It seemed right that there should be no doubts or secrets left to cloud the joy that had come to her this wondrous day.

There was a silence, and she waited, her heart beating its joyous anticipation of something else that Brad must surely tell her very soon . . .

But when he turned his head it was to say: "You'll have heard Kim's news, I take it?"

"Yes," Kate watched the fluttering quest of a huge orange butterfly, "I had a letter at New Year, to tell me a mail-order firm had contracted with a Chinese manufacturer to produce a complete new fashion range exclusive to them, and they'd approached her to do the designs. Oh, and Marda did a big colour feature on her — it's in this month's issue. And Kim had been having the needles again, but so far no miracle," Kate concluded with a sigh of regret.

"Well, I can bring you up to date," Brad said. "A couple of Japanese business men have decided to turn their attention to the rag market. They see no reason why fashion shouldn't follow the transistor and the camera, and a few other things, and they see no reason why Kim's talent should gravitate to the West. So they're going to set Kim up, the whole works, to found an eastern fashion centre to equal anything anywhere else."

"And why not?" said Kate, her eyes thoughtful. "The East has every potential in that line; glorious fabrics, silks, batiks, craftswomen. The West has plundered them for inspiration for years. But I hope they won't exploit Kim," she added doubtfully.

"No more than London or Paris would. And I think Lorna will be keeping a wary eye open in that respect. She's planning to take Kim to the States, to have further medical opinion about that poor little back."

Kate was not surprised to hear this, and she uttered up a fervent little prayer that Lorna's kind-hearted efforts would bring the fulfilment of all their hopes, that Kim might be restored to health and strength once more.

The butterfly came back, hovering above Kate's head, and she stretched out a hand to try to touch its elusive beauty. Then suddenly Brad moved. His outline blotted out sea and sky, and he bent over her.

"Kate, isn't it time we talked about our own future, instead of the pasts and futures of other people?"

"Is it?" She caught at her lower lip as the warmth of his hand came to rest on her thigh. She had not yet come to terms with the power he had to make her aware of the latent potency of her womanhood.

"You know it is." His eyes were insistent. "I'm not prepared to wait very long. How many assignments have you lined up?"

She thought quickly. "Several, I'm afraid. I shall have to honour them, darling."

"I realise that, but how much does this career of yours mean to you? I'm no Victorian chauvinist — heaven forbid that I should ever wish to stifle all your independence of spirit and personality — but I'm not prepared to let my wife spend half her time roving the globe with a rag trade circus, while I spend mine wondering how many men are trying to succeed where I failed for so long," he added vehemently.

"But have you failed?" Kate reached up and wound slim arms round his neck. All her cool reserve was melted now, and the lights of age-old feminine mischief smouldered in her eyes. "Don't you know you're the only man to succeed?"

"For your sake, I'd better stay the only man," he said warningly as he responded to the invitation of those soft arms. "How soon can you be free of commitments?"

"The beginning of May, possibly sooner. I'll have to see Bart first." Kate bit her lip; Bart wasn't going to be very pleased when he heard her news.

"How much time can you salvage during the next two weeks?" he murmured against her ear.

"Almost as much as you want – if you follow me back to London," she tempted.

"London!" he groaned. "Do you think my expense account is made of gold? Oh ... I suppose it'll be worth it. Listen, Kate," he sat up and looked at her with serious eyes, "I'm starting a new job in two weeks' time, in the new technology department at Mahore. And I've bought a house ..."

"I know."

His brows quirked. "The grapevine has long vines. But it's rather a special house ... only you're too big a girl now to live in it. And I'm afraid there wouldn't be room for me."

For long moments she looked into the world of meaning in his eyes. Then she exclaimed: "He told you!"

"Was it a secret?" he asked softly.

"No, not really. Only a long-ago foolish day-dream of a rather foolish little girl."

"I don't think so ..." his eyes had gone very tender. "I think perhaps it was something called predestination, my darling."

Suddenly he dropped back on to the warm silvery sand, reaching out to catch her wrist as he did so and drawing her down to his side. "Come to me soon, Kate, to Mas Pasir, to our little beach and the little shell house I hope our children will play in ... I need you so much."

"Oh, darling ..." She went into his arms, all doubts put far into the past, and all trust into her future in his love.

"But not Mas Pasir," she whispered before his mouth could silence hers. "The first of the thousand sweet returns."

# Romance is Beautiful

Get to the HEART OF HARLEQUIN

**HARLEQUIN READER SERVICE** is your passport to The Heart of Harlequin . . .

# if <u>You</u>...

♥ enjoy the mystery and adventure of romance then you should know that Harlequin is the World's leading publisher of Romantic Fiction novels.

♥ want to keep up to date on all of our new releases, eight brand new Romances and four Harlequin Presents, each month.

♥ are interested in valuable re-issues of best-selling back titles.

♥ are intrigued by exciting, money-saving jumbo volumes.

♥ would like to enjoy North America's unique monthly Magazine "Harlequin" — available **ONLY** through Harlequin Reader Service.

♥ are excited by **anything new** under the Harlequin sun.

# then...

YOU should be on the Harlequin Reader Service — **INFORMATION PLEASE** list — it costs you nothing to receive our news bulletins and intriguing brochures. Please turn page for news of an **EXCITING FREE OFFER.**

# a Special Offer for <u>You</u>...

just by requesting information on Harlequin Reader Service with absolutely no obligation, we will send you a "limited edition" copy, with a new, exciting and distinctive cover design — **VIOLET WINSPEAR'S** first Harlequin Best-Seller

# LUCIFER'S ANGEL

You will be fascinated with this explosive story of the fast-moving, hard-living world of Hollywood in the 50's. It's an unforgettable tale of an innocent young girl who meets and marries a dynamic but ruthless movie producer. It's a gripping novel combining excitement, intrigue, mystery and romance.

A complimentary copy is waiting for YOU — just fill out the coupon on the next page and send it to us to-day.

# Don't Miss...

any of the exciting details of The Harlequin Reader Service—**COLLECTOR'S YEAR** . . .

 It promises to be one of the greatest publishing events in our history and we're certain you'll want to be a part of it.

 Learn all about this great new kind of series.

 Re-issues of some of the earliest, and best-selling Harlequin Romances.

 All presented with a new, exciting and distinctive cover design.

To become a part of the Harlequin Reader Service **INFORMATION PLEASE** list, and to learn more about **COLLECTOR'S YEAR** — simply fill in the coupon below and you will also receive, with no obligation, Violet Winspear's LUCIFER'S ANGEL.